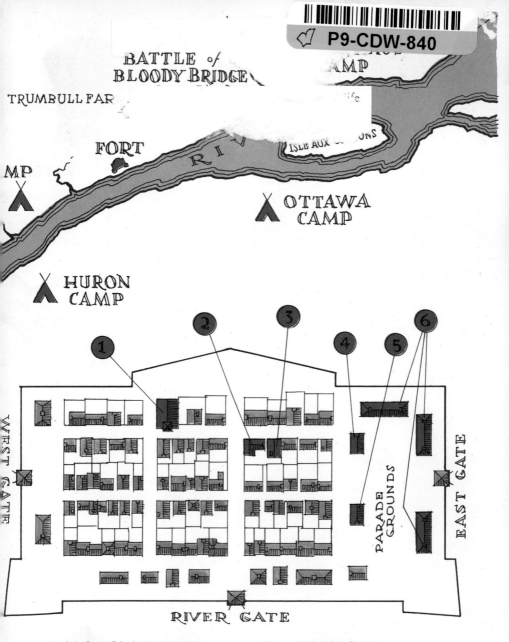

BATTLE of BLOODY BRIDGE

TRUMBULL FAR

CAMP

MP

FORT

RIVER

ISLE AUX ___ONS

OTTAWA CAMP

HURON CAMP

WEST GATE

EAST GATE

PARADE GROUNDS

RIVER GATE

1 ST. ANNE'S CHURCH
2 GIRARD HOUSE & STORE
3 Jᵃˢ STERLING'S STORE
4 Capt. CAMPBELL
5 Maj. GLADWIN
6 BARRACKS

A SPY IN
OLD DETROIT

A SPY in
OLD DETROIT

By Anne Emery

Illustrated by H. B. Vestal

H8561
RAND McNALLY & COMPANY
Chicago   New York   San Francisco

ILLUSTRATIONS

Foreword

THE FRONTIER has always been a world that called to men, and men have always answered that call: brave men, restless men, holy men, greedy men; men who fought the wilderness for gold, for power, for excitement, for curiosity; men who found the challenge of the unknown irresistible; men who went out to conquer and hold new territory for God and for King; and men who followed the leaders.

Such men came from France, with names like Marquette and La Salle and Champlain and Joliet and Cadillac. There were men of God bringing religion to the savages, and men of the world hunting for wealth and fame. In the great inland region of the lakes, they claimed the land for France, befriended the Indians, and outstayed the wilderness.

They built forts to hold their territory, and to trade with the Indians: Presqu'Isle at Erie, Le Boeuf at Waterford, Venango at Franklin, in the Pennsylvania territory; Niagara at the entrance to the Great Lakes waterway at the falls; Pontchartrain du Detroit at the narrow strait between Lakes Erie and Huron; St. Mary's at the entrance to Lake Superior; Michilimackinac at the mouth of Lake Michigan. A chain of forts connected the French colony in the great Louisiana Territory with the French in Canada: Miamis at Fort Wayne, Ouiatenon on the Wabash River near Lafayette, in Indiana; Sandusky near the west end of Lake Erie.

7

And of this chain of forts, Pontchartrain du Detroit, which was built by Antoine Lamotte Cadillac in 1701, grew to be the most important in the region of the lakes, west of Niagara. All the traffic between the fur-trapping western wilderness and the markets of Montreal and Quebec moved through the lakes and straits controlled by Pontchartrain du Detroit.

Because the fort was a trading center, French-speaking Canadian habitants settled there, in little white houses with picket fences, both inside the fort and outside, along the banks of the Detroit River. The fort protected them, and the commandant ruled the settlement as well as the fort. Indians brought their furs to the trading center, and the French invited the Indians to build their villages close by.

From the French explorers and traders, the Indians learned to use steel knives instead of stone, brass kettles instead of clay, steel needles instead of bone. They learned to handle guns, and to love liquor. With muskets and powder, their hunting brought down more game with less work, and they discarded the bows and arrows of their ancestors. They brought in more furs to trade for the white man's riches, and quickly the French grew wealthy and the Indians became dependent.

Indian boys growing up learned to handle guns instead of bows and arrows, and guns needed repairs and ammunition. The Indians needed the French skills, and the French, understanding and liking their savage neighbors, sympathized with their troubles, respected their customs, and became their friends.

As the French came through the St. Lawrence and the lakes from Canada to build more forts and hold more territory in the middle of the New World, British settlers pushed westward across the Appalachian Mountains from the eastern coast. And in 1755 began the long, bloody struggle between them that is now known as the French and Indian War. It was a reflection in the New World of the Seven Years' War in Europe, also between France and England.

When the French governor surrendered to the British major-general Jeffrey Amherst (later Lord Amherst), at Montreal in 1760, French flags came down and British flags were raised in the chain of forts in the heart of North America, from Quebec to the Louisiana line.

As long as the French and the Indians had dwelt and traded together, the French had supplied the Indians with ammunition for their guns, and the Indians had returned their generosity with gifts of venison and furs. Now Amherst, commander in chief of the British forces in North America, decreed that no longer were presents to be given to the Indians. The braves returned from the hunt with their ammunition gone. To refuse them ammunition, was, in their minds, to take bread from their families. They felt that they had been better off under French rule, and were bitter about the British.

Other rebuffs alienated the Indians from their new rulers. The English never respected them as the French had. When a chief died, the French mourned with them and gave them presents to comfort them; the English laughed at their request for condolence. The prices for English goods were higher than they had been when the French held the trading posts; the prices paid for furs were lower. Some of the French were whispering to the Indians that the English secretly planned to wipe them out, and that was why the English kept them short of ammunition. They whispered, too, that the great French Father across the sea was going to send his armies to destroy the English. And it was told across the country that Amherst had given Indian lands to some of his officers. By 1763 the bitter resentment of many tribes was fusing into a hard determination to rid their land of the English and return to French rule.

9

At this time, then, appears the Indian chief Pontiac, who developed a military strategy and a genius for planning a military campaign that no other Indian mind has ever shown. He presented the most formidable Indian resistance the English-speaking people ever faced on this continent.

Within six weeks from the opening of Pontiac's attack on English power in the key fort of Detroit, nine forts fell to the Indians. The only British soldiers left in the entire region of the Great Lakes west of Niagara were the garrison of Fort Detroit, one hundred and forty men under siege by a thousand Indians.

This is a story of that siege.

Chapter 1

WHEN Paul Girard stood in the door of his father's shop in St. Joseph Street, he could look over the stockade of the fort and see the forest and the blue Detroit River. This Friday in late April 1763, was the first true day of spring, and he could smell the pine forest in the warm wind that blew through the fort; he could hear the geese flying northward; and he could see bright clouds running gaily across a brilliant sky. He felt an overpowering need to run wild, to jump and shout and fling himself about in the wild, open space outside the walls.

Paul was fifteen, thin and muscular, happy-go-lucky and carefree, like most of the French-Canadian boys on the wilderness frontier. His father was a successful trader, but today Paul hated trading: counting inventory; trying to please people like his Aunt Louise Cuillerier who always complained about Girard's fabrics; checking orders on a bright day like this, when his brother Philippe was roaming the forests.

Paul admired Philippe intensely. Philippe, who was five years older, had trapped furs with the voyageurs for three winters now, and everyone knew what skill and endurance that required. Philippe had taught Paul to

11

shoot, to sing the songs of the voyageurs, to track like an Indian. Philippe was like an Indian himself.

Last year Philippe had fought off a bear with his fists, and had shown the claw marks to prove it, laughing all the while he talked, his black eyes sparkling as if the wilderness life were all a man could ask for under heaven. Thinking of Philippe now made Paul more hungry for the forest than ever.

Canoes were returning every day and, if the Girard canoe came in, his father would expect him at the river. But Paul told himself he could see the canoe from the willow grove on the river bank, and there had been no customers all afternoon. He locked up the cashbox and asked the English trader next door to keep an eye on the shop while he went on an errand, and then he ran off.

He nodded to the British sentry at the east gate, which stood open, and ran out into the grassy meadowland where a narrow footpath followed the bank of the river. The Detroit was wide and deep, as blue as the sea, and sparkling brilliantly today in the sun. The birch trees were filmy with new leaf, their slim trunks gleaming white among the tall dark pines. Violets poked purple blooms through the forest undergrowth. A chipmunk sat up and stared impudently at Paul as he ran past. And a canoe came around the bend of the river, its red paddles flashing like the wings of a bird as it drove for home. But it was not the Girard canoe, and Paul ran on to the grove, whistling a cardinal's call, to signal the boys to join him.

The willow grove stood at a spot where the shore thrust out into the river, a quarter mile from the fort. It was a group of ancient trees with trunks sloping over the water, big enough to walk on, their trailing branches brushing the water. The leaves were small and new-green, but already they were so thick that one could hide in the upper branches and not be seen. And from this spot Paul could see the Potawatomi village a mile down river, below the fort, the Huron village across from the Potawatomies, and the smoke from the fires of the Ottawa village two miles upstream and across the river from the fort. Paul set his foot against one of the leaning trunks and pulled himself up into the branches by the strong shoots. Three boys were already there, and he settled into a comfortable corner made by a thick branch that stood upright from the trunk.

"What's new with you today?" he said to all three.

Louis La Butte was Paul's cousin. His father was the official interpreter for the Ottawas, and this made Louis feel very important, because his father worked closely with the British commandant of the fort. Now he sat up and puffed out his chest to show that he had something special to tell Paul.

"My father says the Indians are complaining about prices being up again," he announced. "And last week the English laughed at them when they came to say one of their chiefs was dead. They're very angry with the English, and there might be trouble before the summer's over."

Paul looked at his cousin scornfully. "I guess my father

13

trades with as many Indians as your father does. My father isn't worrying about trouble."

"But remember the black rain last October? My father still writes with it. And it smells terrible—like sulphur and brimstone."

Paul sobered in spite of himself. Who could forget that October rain, falling from murky clouds in a midday black as night? But six months had passed since then, and nothing had happened.

"These signs don't wait forever to mean something," he told his cousin.

"When trouble means Indians, it has to wait till they come back from the hunting grounds."

Paul, momentarily silenced, turned to the other boys. Billy Turnbull blew a large cloud of smoke from the peace pipe the boys had captured in a "raid" on an Indian village last summer. He lived with his mother and his older brother on a little farm half a mile north of the fort, on the edge of the forest. He could speak a little French, and he had taught the boys quite a bit of English, and somehow the mixture of languages made his jokes much funnier than they really were. When Billy Turnbull was with them the boys laughed all the time. He was sixteen, blond and blue-eyed, with a stolid air that made his jokes all the more amusing because he delivered them without a smile and always looked surprised at the boys' laughter.

Now he drawled, "I wish you fellows could make up your minds. If the Indians are going on the warpath we ought to know, over there on the farm." He puffed on the peace pipe gravely.

The other three laughed hysterically, and John Rutherfurd reached out to take the peace pipe from Billy.

"I never smoked before," he said, coughing as he swallowed some of the smoke. He drew another mouthful and expelled it without trouble, looked at the peace pipe as if he had conquered something formidable, and gave it back.

John had arrived in Detroit only two weeks earlier, to stay with James Sterling, the trader next door to the Girards. His uncle was Sterling's partner in New York, and John had come to the western lakes to learn something of wilderness trading. He was especially interested in the Indians, of whom he had heard much and so far seen little.

"The greatest luck of my life is this trip to sound the lakes with Lieutenant Robertson," he said now. "You don't really think the Indians are going to rise, do you?" He looked anxiously from one boy to another. Louis looked at Paul, and Paul shook his head, not willing to agree with anything Louis said.

"Oh, I don't think they'll rise very soon," he said.

The sound of a homecoming voyageur song came across the water, and Paul sat up straight, parting the leaves to look toward the landing place outside the fort.

"That looks like our canoe," he said, beginning to slide down the trunk of the tree. He stopped halfway down and looked up at the boys persuasively. "Come on and

15

help us to haul the stuff. We will need a lot of hands."

"Don't mind if I do." Billy dangled from a branch, pipe in mouth, and dropped to the ground. The others followed, and the boys raced each other to the fort, where they followed the path outside the walls to the sandy beach before the water gate.

Two armed vessels, the sloop *Michigan* and the *Huron,* stood at anchor in the river, at each corner of the stockade. Their crews were hanging over the rail, observing the incoming canoe with as much interest as the habitants who had gathered along the shore. As the first voyageur stepped out of the canoe upon the sand, a cheer went up from first one ship and then the other. The crowd yelled in greeting, and then surged down upon the sand. Some curious Indians were among them, watching as eagerly as the settlers to see what the canoe brought back from the winter's hunt.

As far back as Paul could remember, the Indians had had their summer villages along the banks of the river near the fort. He knew their mud and wattle huts as well as he knew the neat, white, thatched cottages of his French neighbors.

Otussa was among the Indians who were watching the trappers. He was a young Ottawa, a couple of years older than Paul, and the two boys had played together for years. He had taught Paul how to wrestle so well that every once in a while Paul could overcome him. He had shown him how to fish and trap in the Indian way. The boys had raced in the meadow until Paul matched Otussa's speed, and Paul considered Otussa one of his best friends.

Otussa's father was one of the Ottawa chiefs, and the boy wanted more than anything else to be a chief himself some day. Chiefs must be stronger, braver, more heroic than other men, and Otussa had worked toward this ambition since he was small. Rarely did he laugh or chatter as Paul's French and English friends did. For him life was very serious.

Now Otussa looked around, saw Paul, and acknowledged him with a slight gesture. Paul waved to the Indian and pushed his way through the crowd and down to the water's edge. Then he gave a shrill whoop. The Girard canoe had come in, and Philippe was home.

The voyageurs were already unloading the big canoe, tossing jokes at the crowd, and laughing about being home again, after the long, hard winter. They were short, stocky men, hardy and tough, who spent their lives trapping for the fur traders. But they were gay and carefree, loving their life in the forests, wild as Indians.

Philippe turned eagerly toward the waiting crowd. His eyes were bright and his smile was dazzling in his dark face. He wore the deerskin leggings, bright sash, and red cap of the voyageur, and he tossed his head and strutted like a homecoming conqueror. Paul threw himself upon his brother and embraced him. Philippe held him at arm's length and looked him over.

"My little brother," he said, as if he couldn't believe it.

17

"How you've grown this winter while I've been gone!"

Their father reached the sandy strip and embraced Philippe; and then he held him off with both hands on his arms, looking pridefully at his homecoming son. "How was the trapping, my boy? It seemed like a long winter while you were gone."

"We got fine furs, my father." Philippe smiled proudly and lifted his head like an eagle. "It's good to be home again. How is my mother?"

"She awaits you impatiently." His father slapped him on the shoulder. "Go to her, Philippe. We'll get the furs moved."

Philippe moved away through the crowd with springing steps, and his father looked at Paul, scowling.

"You, Paul!" he yelled. "Why weren't you at the store when I sent for you?"

Paul stood respectfully, head lowered, while his father berated him. "I went to get the boys to help me," he said, waving toward his friends. Louis and Billy stepped forward and picked up one of the heavy bundles of furs.

"Ah, well," his father conceded, "it's good to have the extra hands. I thought you'd forgotten the canoe was expected today."

"How could I forget?" Paul cried, looking at Billy. The English boy winked at him solemnly, and Paul had to choke back another burst of laughter, as Billy and Louis hoisted their load and began to move it up the narrow street. He and John Rutherfurd picked up another bundle

Paul threw himself upon his brother and embraced him

and followed. The ground in the fort sloped up from the river, and St. Joseph Street was farthest from the water gate, and all uphill.

The Girard store was a good-sized room, with a counter, a few shelves, and light coming through small-paned windows. Back of the store was the family's home: a living room, dining room, and tiny kitchen, and a bedroom for the father and mother. Up a narrow, steep flight of stairs were two more bedrooms, under the steeply sloping roof: one for the two girls, one for the four boys.

In the small courtyard was a tiny herb garden and a chicken yard in a corner near the kitchen, where a dozen hens and a flock of small yellow chicks pecked busily all day. The warehouse ran across the back of the courtyard. It was a barnlike building seventy feet long, with shuttered windows looking out upon the fifteen-foot stockade wall on the northwest side of the fort, and a small stable at one end, where the Girard's two cows could be sheltered when they were brought inside the fort from pasture at night.

The boys carried the heavy loads of furs through the courtyard gate and into the warehouse, and put them on the long table. As Henri Girard began to cut the rawhide thongs from the first bundle, Louis, Billy, and John disappeared before anyone could ask them to do any more work. But Paul watched his father, as interested in the quality of the pelts as the trader himself.

There were raccoon pelts, mink, otter, buckskins, and

a goodly proportion of the most highly valued, beaver.

"These," Monsieur Girard said, as he picked up a bundle of beaver pelts, "these should please even Monsieur Cuillerier. Fah! That snob! He must have the finest of everything, even if he has to buy from another trader than me, his own brother-in-law!"

He tossed the prime pelts into a corner as if he despised them as much as the man who would buy them. Uncle Antoine Cuillerier was richer, more opinionated, and more arrogant than anyone else in Detroit. His half brother had been commandant of the fort before the English came, and now Antoine Cuillerier thought the community belonged to him.

"When the English leave," he had said openly, "and they will leave, I will be the next commandant."

"He should keep his mouth shut," Paul's other uncle, Pierre La Butte, had growled. "The English are not going to leave, and I don't know why he talks in this foolish fashion."

"He says the Indians hate the English," Paul had said.

"And so they may. But the Indians aren't going to decide a thing like that. The English are here to stay. We've sworn allegiance to their king. I don't like him, but I will not betray my sworn oath, even so."

A man's oath was a sacred thing, Paul's father had taught him long ago. On the day the British had taken over the fort, the French had been sworn en masse to British allegiance. Paul had not opened his mouth. But he was young and hardly aware of what the British officer was saying.

Uncle Pierre La Butte had sworn to be loyal to the British command, and he considered himself bound by that oath. Philippe had stood silent and scowling, and considered himself bound to no man. He always said he had a right to choose his own obedience and loyalty, and would not be bound by someone else's ideas.

When he thought about it, Paul found himself divided between admiring Uncle Pierre for his uncompromising principle and Philippe for his independence. But Uncle Antoine was different. He had stood up there and sworn as loudly as anyone. And now, two and a half years later, he talked equally loudly with his French friends about taking over the fort from the English. Paul disapproved of Uncle Antoine as much as his father did. He had not the sense of honor a Frenchman should have.

Thinking of his Uncle Antoine, Paul straightened up and stretched. Through the open door he could hear the cries of a little girl playing with her dog, the chatter of the women down at the pump in the center of the fort, the shouted orders of the English drill sergeant on the parade ground. Life was pleasant here in Fort Detroit, and why should one care about the French king overseas, whom no one in Detroit had even seen, or the English king, either?

Two and a half years ago the English had taken command of the fort, and the French had watched, some of them weeping, while the blue flag with the lilies of France had come down the staff of Fort Pontchartrain, and the red flag with the cross of St. George of England had soared up to snap in the cold wind across the fort that would now be called Fort Detroit. Paul remembered the dismay and the weeping, and now he wondered why it had mattered so much.

He had come to know many of the English in those years. There were a couple of youths in the garrison who were about Philippe's age—Jack Bradshaw and Tom Smith. He spent quite a lot of time with them, learning English, hearing interesting things about their military life, listening to their stories of life back home. Both had been homesick those first months, and Paul had discovered that the English boys were very much like his French friends. After the garrison had been in the fort two and a half years, it seemed as if they had been there always. Jack felt as Paul did, that in this new land kings did not matter much.

This is our land, Paul thought now, looking beyond the stockade across the blue river and the open fields to the endless forests. This place has nothing to do with kings. My family helped to build Detroit, and it belongs to us, to me. No king has anything to say to us.

His father locked up the warehouse, and they went into the house to see Philippe. The voyageur was telling stories of the winter adventures to his younger brothers, and they were listening with eyes glowing and mouths open. His mother watched him with a warm tenderness in her eyes.

"And that's how I brought down that elk," he ended, looking up as Paul came in. "Biggest one you ever saw ... Paul, how about going down to the parade ground before supper? I want to see some of the boys."

The parade ground was filled with boys and young men, English and French, and a shout of welcome went up as Philippe appeared.

"Here's John Rutherfurd!" Paul cried. "He wants to meet a voyageur, Philippe."

John looked up from the group about him, and the two shook hands, looking at each other with interest. Philippe was small, like all voyageurs, but he had enormous shoulders and an air of cocky confidence. John Rutherfurd was tall and friendly.

"I've wanted to meet a voyageur ever since I came out from New York. "What a great life you must have!"

Philippe threw out his chest and acknowledged this recognition with satisfaction. "I like the wilderness."

"I, too!" John said. He turned back to his audience, including Philippe now. "As I was saying about this trip through the lakes, they tell me the sport should be magnificent. Especially the waterfowl. We'll be a good-sized party: six soldiers, two sailors, besides Lieutenant Charles Robertson and Sir Robert Davers and his Pawnee slave."

"Will you tell me why a man like Davers comes to a place like this?" Alexis Cuillerier asked, jestingly.

Paul's cousin Alexis was an arrogant young man in his

middle twenties, and Paul alternately admired and detested him. Now Paul laughed with the others at the thought of Davers, the middle-aged English tourist, poking around in the wilderness in the middle of the New World.

"He wants to see the world." Rutherfurd winked at Paul as he answered Alexis. "He's been learning Indian languages, and he thinks this chance to see the lakes is a great thing." He laughed. "Of course, I think it's a great thing, too. But I'm seventeen, and Davers must be forty. However, he's spry and active. Good company, really."

"Do you think the Indians will give you any trouble?" one of the youths asked.

"Oh, not a bit! Why should they?" he said confidently. "They seem like friendly chaps, and Davers can speak their language now."

Alexis looked at him from under dark brows, and then across at Philippe. Paul felt a warning in the air, almost as tangible as a cold wind.

"Alexis," he said sharply. His cousin looked at him coldly. "Do you know anything about trouble with the Indians?"

Alexis dropped his eyes as if he had dropped a shutter to close out the light.

"Not a thing." He shook his head.

But Paul knew he lied, and he dared not look at Philippe. Something ugly was going to happen, and Alexis Cuillerier knew what it was.

Chapter 2

THE Girards celebrated Philippe's return with the finest dinner Marie Girard could put together. Marie sat at the head of her table and looked upon her family with fond pride. She was plump and dark and energetic, with a mobile face that was sometimes plain, sometimes wistful, and almost pretty tonight, because she was happy. She was renowned for her excellent cooking, and for this dinner for her homecoming son she had outdone herself: fine whitefish, a salad of dandelion greens and dried herbs from her kitchen garden, roast goose, hot crusty bread, and a cream pastry for dessert. She had the lightest hand for pastry of any of the wives in the settlement.

Philippe sat beside his mother, and his eyes gleamed at the food. His sister Suzette sat next to him. She was sixteen, with blond hair and dark eyes, a demure young lady, quiet and well-bred. She spoke little, being dreamy much of the time. Robert, one of the ten-year-old twins, sat next to Suzette. Charles, the other twin, sat on the other side of the table. The boys were separated at meals because they scuffled so much. Paul was between Charles and Félice, the seven-year-old sister. Félice had brought her doll to the table, and when her father ordered her to take it away again, her eyes filled with tears, and she comforted the doll at great length before she left her in a corner.

Philippe settled back after the dinner, sighing with satisfaction. "You must have known we had nothing to eat all winter but pemmican."

"I know, and so unnecessary. Why must you go into the wilderness like that, Philippe? Can't you stay home now?"

"I've just come home," he said lightly. "Of course I'll stay—for awhile."

His father looked at him sharply. Mme. Girard gestured with her hand. Paul knew what that gesture meant: "Let's not have an argument at the dinner table!" She said quickly, "Will you have another bit of the pastry, Philippe? I made it just for your homecoming."

But Philippe shook his head. "I'll save it for tomorrow, Mother. I've eaten too much as it is. Tell me about our friends."

For an hour they talked amicably about their neighbors. Marie-Francoise Navarre was marrying the English lieutenant McDougall, on the sixth of May, and the Navarres were having a great party to celebrate the wedding. Philippe looked angry and sad, but he said nothing. The English trader, James Sterling, was courting Angélique Cuillerier, and how did her father feel about that? The priest at Ste. Anne's Church, Father Bocquet, had declared that Paul should go to Montreal for study, and Paul didn't want to go. It was said the Indians were growing restless, and some of the habitants were alarmed.

"And well they might be restless," Philippe said impatiently. "The English have treated the Indians so badly it will be no surprise to me if the Indians try to wipe them all out."

"That's just what I said," Mme. Girard cried triumphantly. "When we had that black rain last October—do you remember, Philippe?—I said it meant great trouble."

Philippe nodded. "Of course it meant trouble. Anyone knows a sign like that is important." He stretched lustily, tipping his chair back from the table, and then he sat up straight again.

"I'm going to sleep with the Ottawas tonight," he announced.

"But you have just come home!" his mother cried.

"I know. But I've lived in the forests too much to live inside these walls now, strangled by the English."

"Do not be ridiculous!" his father said sharply. "A man can't spend his life wandering around like a savage."

"I can!" Philippe cried. "A man like me can't spend his life cooped up in a little stockade! How can you submit to the English like this? Have you no spirit, Father? What are you living for?"

"I'm not living to fight," his father told him tartly. Both men were on their feet glowering at each other, and Mme. Girard clasped her hands and looked despairingly from one to the other.

"Your life is yours to live, not mine," Henri Girard cried. "But I tell you, you talk like a fool!"

28

Philippe flung himself out of the house with a muttered oath, and his mother wrung her hands. "Henri! Do not blame the boy. He is young, he doesn't know what he says." She made sweeping motions with both hands toward the younger children. "Charles! Robert! Go out and bring in the cows. Félice, look to the chickens!"

As the younger children disappeared, Henri Girard stiffened his back and said, "I was just as foolish at his age." He sounded annoyed with the boy he had been. "Why should he make the same mistakes if I can keep him from them?"

"But how will he learn without mistakes? Philippe will let no one tell him anything."

"Who will help with the business? Is the boy mad, that he has no thought for the future?"

"Tchch," said his wife. "What is there to think of the future, except that it will some day be here? Paul can be the trader instead of Philippe. He should go to Montreal, as the good father says. And how can one know what to plan? For two years now Philippe has brought back better furs than Sterling's engagés."

"And he grows closer to the Indians with each year. Where will this end? Will he be a voyageur all his life?"

"I'd like to go with him next fall," Paul said.

His father glared at him. "You will learn how to trade," he told him. "Why do you think Father Bocquet has been giving you schooling?"

Why indeed? Paul had often wondered, rebelliously.

He hated studying, and only four of the boys in the settlement were getting formal learning. Why, when all he wanted was to roam the wilderness and explore the forest, should he be sitting through stifling hours of reading, figuring, writing, learning to spell? He had argued the question with his father too many times already, and now he wished he had gone with Philippe to the Ottawa camp. He sighed with the difficulties of pleasing both his parents and himself. Just then some neighbors came in to chat about the Navarre wedding and the English officers, and Paul forgot his anger in the gaiety of the company.

But the next morning when Paul went to work in the store again his gloom returned. The stocks of goods were almost exhausted, and his father was counting what was left. Paul refolded and arranged the fine blankets from France and England, and the coarse blankets, or strouds, in which the Indians wrapped themselves. He tallied boxes of worsted hose, bolts of flowered serge, calico, calimanco cloth, and he hated every minute of it. Nothing, he was thinking, his mouth tightened over clamped teeth, nothing could make him be a trader when the wilderness called as it did today. When he was a man, he, too, would be free like Philippe....

Two Ottawas entered the store, bearing part of their winter's catch. Silently the taller one flung the furs upon the counter.

"How much?" he asked in a guttural voice.

Henri Girard gestured to Paul to deal with the trappers.

The shorter Ottawa picked up a scarlet stroud

Paul knew these men, as he knew almost everyone in the
Ottawa tribe. He greeted them pleasantly and counted the
furs: forty raccoons, thirty beavers, ten buckskins. He told
off the count and the Indians nodded. The shorter one
picked up a scarlet stroud.

"Three beavers," Paul told him.

The man threw down the stroud, scowling fiercely.

"Too much!" he ejaculated. "When the French commandant held this fort we got strouds for two beavers. How much for gunpowder?"

"One pound, one beaver. That's the English price." Paul sounded apologetic.

The Indians looked darkly at him, and then at each other.

"The English do not keep their promises," the taller one cried in a rage. "They promise lower prices, they ask higher. They promise ammunition, they give us none. Our powder is gone, we can't bring enough furs to buy powder. Our families will be hungry!"

Henri Girard came forward and spoke soothingly. He told the Indians that the English did not understand and some time they might change. But they had set the prices, and all must obey their rule. He praised the quality of the skins they had brought in and offered a little better price on what they wanted to buy. Looking more content, the Indians selected strouds, shirts, and clasp knives. They bought tobacco, and each chose a tomahawk, hefting several for weight and balance before they were satisfied. Girard totaled up the cost of their purchases and showed them the credit for the remaining furs. And then he gave each of them a small box of wampum beads, a bar of lead, and a couple of pounds of powder. They looked happier, but still they went out grumbling.

"They're pretty angry with the English," Paul said, watching them go out the door muttering to each other.

"The English are fools," his father said impatiently. "They irritate the Indians uselessly." He shook his head. "If trouble comes, the English will have brought it upon themselves." It was the third time in two days that Paul had heard that frightening prediction.

His father turned briskly toward the warehouse, as if he were putting out of his mind any fears for the English. "Lieutenant Robertson has said he can deliver that flour for Monsieur Desnoyers," he said. "They'll be going right past the Pinery. It should go on the bateau tomorrow. Better take it down there now."

Glad for a reason to be outdoors, Paul rolled a barrel of flour down to the water gate, and found Sir Robert Davers discussing the trip with Lieutenant Robertson.

"I see no reason for fearing an Indian attack," Sir Robert was saying confidently, as Paul rolled the flour barrel into place on the sand. "I've been talking with some of the savages—I speak their language, you know—and they're quite friendly, really."

Lieutenant Robertson nodded. "I quite agree with you, Sir Robert. Nothing to fear at all."

Paul walked back up the sloping street for the second barrel, slowly and thoughtfully. The English were so confident that nothing could happen. And yet he could not forget the gloomy predictions he had been hearing. He wished there were some way to know . . .

Sunday, the first of May, was a bright, fair day, and

Philippe came home to attend mass with his family. They could see the white spire of Ste. Anne's Church shining in the sunlight as they left their home. The twins took care of Félice who carried her doll to church. Félice liked to dawdle. During the service she ordered her *poupette* to pay close attention to the prayers. She herself was demure and quiet, her bright eyes glancing from one to another of her brothers.

Philippe sat between Paul and Suzette in his voyageur costume, and his voice sang out above the others. Admiring eyes turned toward him, and his mother preened herself at the attention paid to her eldest son. His father sat stiffly dignified, ignoring all of it.

After the service the Girards visited with their friends in the sunny square before the church. Paul and Philippe joined the boys and young men on the parade ground, and listened to John Rutherfurd talking again about his trip and drawing in the sandy ground with a pointed stick as he talked.

"We'll move up the Detroit River to Lake St. Clair," he said, "leave the flour for Desnoyers at the Pinery, in three days, maybe four. Then we go up through Lake Huron, all the way to Michilimackinac. I daresay we won't be back here for a month or more." He looked up as Paul leaned over to see his diagram. "Say, Paul!" His eyes snapped with excitement. "Know what I want to do next? Maybe we could go with some voyageurs next fall!"

Both boys looked at Philippe, who threw out his chest

and laughed aloud. "You think it's easy to be a voyageur, *hein*? I should show you!"

"Oh, I know it's not easy," John agreed. "But exciting, isn't it? I'm going all the way to the Western Ocean some day."

"That's what I want to see!" Billy Turnbull cried. He was always talking about exploring the rivers that ran to the western seas, through unknown western mountains. Paul began eagerly planning a trip of exploration with Billy and Louis La Butte, and Philippe moved a little away to talk with his cousin Alexis.

"What's the new Englishman doing here?" He glanced toward Rutherfurd.

"He's visiting Sterling, learning the trading business," Alexis told him, sneering a little.

"Ah? And does he plan to stay—after this lake trip?"

"Who knows?"

"Seems pleasant enough."

"Oh, yes. If you like the English..."

And then all the young men turned toward the gate as a clamorous noise sounded outside the wall. They could see a large crowd of Indians outside the open gate, and the sentry yelled as if he were repeating something he'd said a number of times: "Major Gladwin's orders! No Indians come in the fort today!"

John Rutherfurd stood up straight and looked toward the gate.

"I wish he'd let them in," he muttered. "I haven't seen

No Indians come in the fort today!

nearly as much of the Indians as I hoped to when I came out here."

An arrogant Indian voice was demanding Monsieur La Butte.

"That's Pontiac!" Louis said. He ran to the gate.

"Hey, you, ain't you La Butte's boy?" the sentry asked.

Louis nodded. "Greetings, my brother," he said to Pontiac in the Ottawa tongue. "Is there trouble?"

Before Pontiac could reply, the sentry said, "He wants your father. Wants to talk about not coming in, I guess."

He laughed as if he had said something very funny. Louis stared coldly at the sentry as if he could find nothing to laugh at, and then he turned again to Pontiac. "I will bring my father at once, great chief."

Paul and the boys waited while Louis ran to his father's house. Paul had seen Pontiac before, because the chief came often to the fort. But today, because of the rumors that had been flying around, he seemed to look different. Paul told himself he was just looking for trouble because he'd heard so many tales. But still . . .

The Ottawa chief stood before the gate so arrogantly, his frame was so strong and muscular, his motions so smooth and easy, that he gave the impression of great power. Behind him the crowding braves were murmuring angrily. Pontiac lifted his head and stared at the sentry, until the soldier was embarrassed and shifted his eyes to Paul.

"These Indians been coming and going all this time," he

complained. "Today we get orders, don't let 'em in. What am I supposed to do?"

The young Frenchmen were silently observing the business at the gate, smiling to each other at the sentry's embarrassment. As La Butte approached, the sentry let out a sigh of relief. "He can tell us what's going on."

Philippe stared at the sentry angrily, and muttered with an oath, in French, "These English! No wonder the Indians hate them. Look at that dog of a sentry: he speaks to a great chief as if he were a slave! Why should Pontiac take that? His people were here hundreds of years before the English came with their pompous greed. If I were Pontiac, I'd spit in his face!"

He raised his voice as if he wanted the sentry to know how he felt. But the sentry ignored the French he could not understand, and listened to the interpreter in open-mouthed amusement at the deference the Frenchman showed to the Indian.

La Butte looked like an Indian himself, dark, stolid, unsmiling. He had lived with the Indians in his youth. Now he spoke first to Pontiac, and then turned to translate for the sentry.

"Chief Pontiac says he has brought his men to entertain the commandant. They wish to dance the calumet for him."

"Orders is orders," the sentry repeated stolidly.

"Very well." The interpreter spoke to Pontiac again, and went across the way to the house of Major Henry

Gladwin, the commandant, while the Indians stirred restlessly. When he returned five minutes later he gave the sentry a note from the commandant. The sentry saluted, lowered his musket, and stepped to one side of the great gate. Pontiac moved majestically through the opening without a glance at any of the white men about him, and led his braves into the open space before the house of the commandant, where the English officers stood at attention to greet them.

"Magnificent, aren't they?" John Rutherfurd turned to Paul and Louis. "This is the first time since I came from New York that I've seen Indians like this!"

Forty warriors, bronzed and shining, danced in a sinuous circle, stooping and then stretching upright, their feet drumming the ground in an intricate rhythm. They danced with chanting cries, beating upon a post in the center of the circle, and then breaking into singsong recitation.

Paul listened to the chant, and he felt cold. Each warrior sang of his victories, his great battles, his unconquerable strength, and they proclaimed, "We have beaten the English many times, and we shall beat them again." The tranquillity and courteous attention of the English officers showed that they understood nothing of the Indian chant.

"The calumet is the peace-pipe dance," Paul told John. "It's a compliment to dance it for the garrison."

But he had never heard the accompanying words sound so threatening, and he looked beyond the dancers. Ten of the warriors had slipped away and were walking in the streets of the fort. While his friends watched the dance, Paul moved quietly away and strolled up the street toward his father's store. The Indians walked in twos and threes, erect, businesslike, staring at every house. They studied the shops with special interest. Paul came up and spoke to them cheerfully in the Indian tongue. They ignored his greeting, watching him silently until he had passed. Looking back as he turned a corner, he saw that they were peering into the window of the powder magazine, counting.

Slowly he walked back to the dance.

"I wish you weren't going on this trip into the lakes tomorrow," he said to John Rutherfurd. "The Indians aren't friendly just now."

Rutherfurd looked at him in surprise. "Oh, come now. They've made no trouble for years. And you said yourself that the calumet they offer today is the peace-pipe dance."

"It could be a ruse," Paul said unhappily.

Rutherfurd laughed at his fears. "We're traveling with soldiers and arms. There's nothing to fear, nothing at all! An attack would be an interesting experience, and I welcome experiences . . . " He watched the dancers another moment. "But there's not a chance of Indian trouble now."

Chapter 3

THE Robertson expedition set off on their trip to sound the lakes on Monday, and Paul was down at the waterfront to wave them off. The day was warm and sunny, and the wilderness called him. When the bateau had disappeared around the curve of the river, he walked slowly back up the hill to the store and brooded about the life he faced.

John was going on a great adventure; Philippe was free to live where he chose and do as he liked. And he, Paul, was tied to his father's plans for his future, condemned to be a storekeeper all his life. He hated it, he told himself, as he went into the warehouse, that was dim even on the brightest days, and hunted for the goods his father had told him to bring to the store and display for sale. He was bored and exasperated with the routine work of the trader. He wanted in some way to prove himself, to be a hero; he craved a challenge that would test his courage.

Otussa craved that same challenge, he recalled. Otussa wanted, more than anything else in the world, to be a brave and then a chief. He remembered the day Otussa had told him his ambition. The Indian's eyes had burned with a cold, glittering fire that was chilling in its intensity.

"Some day I, too, will be a great chief," he had said. "Like Pontiac, like Wabbicomigot, or Wasson. For this I prepare for battle where I can prove myself."

In the courtyard Paul heard the hens squawking and the chicks chittering madly. He stepped out to see what was going on. A hawk's shadow sailed in slow circles over the henyard, and the tiny yellow chicks skittered around hunting shelter. He grinned at their panic. But the shadow of the hawk fell over his own spirit, and, looking up, he thought the sailing menace looked like Otussa. He went back into the warehouse slowly, thoughtfully.

"The stocks are so low there's nothing to do," his father said grumpily. "If that shipment doesn't come in from Niagara we'll have to close up in a week. Run along— take this package to Uncle Antoine. You might as well run off some energy."

Paul raced through the narrow streets and out of the east gate before his father should change his mind. And then he decided to circle around by Billy Turnbull's house.

Billy's father had died a few months after he had brought his family out to this farm in the wilderness, and Billy and his older brother had been taking care of the farm for their mother since then. Mrs. Turnbull was an energetic woman who once had told Paul that she liked living away from the rest of the settlement.

"I don't like to be in the middle of people," she had said; "that's one reason we came out here."

She always seemed glad to see Paul, and often she gave him fragrant dark gingerbread. She was different from the French women who were his mother's friends, but Paul liked her very much.

Billy was plowing the south field back of the house, and he waved as Paul approached.

"I'm going upriver a little way to give this package to Uncle Antoine," Paul said. "Come along."

Billy shook his head. "I've got to finish plowing. We're late this year. Next week I could get away. How about some fishing then?"

Paul watched him turn his ox into the next furrow. The lazy gait of the ox in the plow shafts, the rich, brown earth turning in heavy furrows, gave him a feeling of deep satisfaction. Beyond the plowed land the apple trees were pink with buds. Along the fence by the house the wild grapes were in full leaf. He was filled with a sense of well-being. Life in this wilderness of the lakes was very sweet.

"We'll go fishing next week, then," he called, with a wave, and he moved on down the rough path that angled toward the Cuilleriers' house on the river bank a half mile away. Under his feet the moss was thick and springy. He slowed down and made no haste to finish his errand.

When he reached his Uncle Antoine's house, Philippe was sitting with his uncle and his cousin Alexis. He looked up, saw Paul, and there was a sudden silence. Paul gave his uncle the package.

"Oh, yes. Thanks very much." Uncle Antoine sounded as if he'd forgotten the order, as if his thoughts were far away. "Sit down, sit down, Paul," he said at last.

Paul looked from one to the other. He disliked Uncle Antoine as much as his father did. But still, Philippe was here. Paul was about to join them when he looked at Alexis. His cousin looked bored and angry with the interruptions, and suddenly Paul knew he didn't really want to stay.

"Thank you just the same, Uncle Antoine, I must get home again."

Philippe got up lazily and held out a packet wrapped in leaves. "I brought this sugar from the Ottawa camp. Take it to Mother, and tell her I'll come home and see her on Friday."

Paul felt strangely awkward and intrusive in his uncle's presence. No one had much to say while he stood there. He made his farewells and started back on the river path, feeling their eyes on him as he went.

Cousin Alexis was going to be just like Uncle Antoine some day, he thought, as he left the settlement behind. He was a wild, bullying young man, who constantly made trouble, and Uncle Antoine was an arrogant, bullying old man, who also made trouble. The thought cheered him up so much that he whistled all the way back to the fort. He remembered that Philippe had said he was coming home on Friday, and he wondered if it was because of the Navarre wedding that night.

On Friday it rained all day long. Spirits were depressed, tempers were ragged, and the long-overdue shipment of goods for the merchants arrived in the downpour and was unloaded and left standing in the pouring rain.

Paul worked all morning carrying boxes and bales from the landing place to the warehouse. At noon Philippe arrived.

"So you come at last," his father greeted him. "It's about time. Why can you not give me more help with the store?"

Philippe stood carelessly leaning against the wall of the warehouse. He looked at his father patiently and courteously, swinging a chain in a circle as if he listened without hearing.

"I'm sorry to grieve you, Father. But when I come inside this fort I choke for air—" His dark eyes blazed. "You don't know how it feels, that freedom of the wild! The forests, the sunsets, the free-running streams, the open fires at night—" He flung his arms wide as if he appealed for understanding. Then he smiled at his father teasingly. "You, yourself—why did you come to this wilderness of the lakes at seventeen, when you lived in a fine city like Montreal?"

His father scowled and then, unwillingly, a smile twitched at his mouth as if he recalled a long-gone memory. "Sometimes I wonder why I did . . . " He turned away impatiently. "Now that you're here, you can help get those goods off the shore. Some of them are still standing in the rain."

Philippe accompanied Paul and his father through the rain. The crew had covered most of the boxes and barrels with tarpaulins, but some of the Girard shipment had become uncovered.

Major Gladwin's aide, disgruntled with the water trickling inside his collar, was at the landing place. As Paul began stacking a load of small boxes for the next trip to the warehouse, he heard the aide talking to the ship's captain.

"We've been looking for a shipment for the garrison for days," he said. "We've needed food and ammunition for weeks. Do you know anything about a ship from Niagara for the garrison?"

The captain shook his head. "Haven't seen anything like that," he said dourly. "Indians giving us a lot of trouble these days. Maybe they held up the major's shipment along the way."

"What's gotten into the Indians?" the aide demanded irritably. He turned away, hunching his shoulders in the rain, and splashed back through the running streams of water into the fort.

Philippe nodded after him. "Maybe they'll all starve," he said hopefully. "It might be the easiest way after all to get rid of the English."

"But why should you feel like that?" Paul demanded. "I know many of the English, and they're fine people."

"I'll tell you why I hate the English," Philippe said between his teeth. He hoisted a barrel of gunpowder to his shoulder as easily as if it had been feathers, and turned to stride up the street with it. Paul lifted his pile of boxes of woolen hose with effort, and followed his brother, admiring the easy strength with which he carried the heavy barrel. Philippe waited for him at the corner, and the two fell into step together.

"The English know nothing of the Indians," Philippe said angrily. "They treat them like inferiors, like savages. The Indians are savage, yes. But they have the finest qualities of natural man: they are brave, they are proud, and they love liberty even more than we do. Liberty and glory—for these an Indian will fight and die. And so would I . . . "

"But the English want only peace and friendship," Paul protested. "Perhaps they make mistakes, but so does everyone. So did we French."

"They don't want friendship," Philippe said coldly. "They want conquest. They will rule this New World, and where will we French be then? This has been our world for two centuries, and now the English take it and push us aside—"

"Not if we join with them in building the New World! They want us to be friends. And what does any government on the other side of the ocean mean to us here? Why can't we live in peace with the English and the Indians, here in Detroit? Why must we fight here, for a faraway king?"

They had reached the warehouse, and Philippe swung

Paul lifted his pile of boxes and followed his brother

his heavy load to the ground as easily as he had picked it up. Paul let his down slowly.

"We'll have to fight," Philippe said darkly, "because the English are goading the Indians into it. If the English build colonies, the Indians will lose their hunting grounds. They will fight to prevent this. And when war comes, it's our great chance to get rid of the English and rule this territory again as Frenchmen. We can live with our Indian brothers, and the English cannot."

Paul looked at his brother, and their glances locked. "You think there will be fighting, then?"

"I know it."

The two turned back to carry more loads from the river bank, and for a long time they said no more. The water ran from St. Joseph Street in rushing little rivulets through the lanes that led down to the waterfront. In the gloomy day the fort was dark and somber. Paul thought about his brother's words, trying not to believe them. If there was fighting . . . But he did not want to think of fighting.

To forget that ugly threat, he asked, "Will you go to the Navarre wedding with us tonight?"

Philippe looked away, and his face hardened. "Not I. There is no wedding I should dislike more to see."

Of course, Paul thought, in swift regret that he had spoken. His mother had said more than once that she blamed the Navarre girl for Philippe's determination to live in the forest with the Indians. And now she was marrying an English officer . . . No wonder Philippe hated the English. When the last load was stored in the warehouse, Philippe glanced toward his father, working in a distant corner, and spoke quietly to Paul.

"I'm going back now. Just tell Father when he asks that I'll be in the fort again before very long."

He went as silently as an Indian, and Paul worked quickly to finish checking the inventory before the day ended. A brilliant and surprising ray of sunlight fell across the floor, and Paul, startled, straightened up, feeling his muscles ache from the stooping and carrying he had been doing. He went to the door to breathe the fresh air.

The rain had stopped, and the clear blue sky in the west was shading into hazy gold. The sun was sinking now, its long golden rays turning the wet streets to iridescence. Below the black and purple clouds, the golden horizon turned to scarlet, the forests grew black in the fading sunlight. Paul thought the change in the weather must be a good omen.

Mme. Girard rejoiced volubly in the beautiful weather, as she dressed her family in silks and laces for the Navarre wedding. Marie-Francoise Navarre's betrothal to Lieutenant George McDougall, of the English garrison, was deeply interesting to the habitants. The lieutenant had come to Detroit only two years ago, and Marie-Francoise had been throwing herself at his head ever since, gossip said. Well, now she was marrying the man.

"But can you tell me," Mme. Girard demanded of her husband, as the family set out for the Navarre house outside the walls, where the ceremony would take place, "what she can see in that Englishman, when she might have had a fine young Frenchman like our Philippe?"

Her husband could not tell her. The stars were beginning to show, the frogs along the river bank gurgled lustily, and the fresh scents of the rain-washed evening arose along the river path, as they left the walls of the fort behind them. Mme. Navarre chattered on. She would not have gone one step to this wedding, save that the Navarres were old friends, and everyone in the village would be there.

Paul walked along reluctantly, resenting the wedding too. He hated to dress up, already his starched shirt was chafing his neck. He wished again that he could go off with Philippe and forget the fort and its problems.

Chapter 4

THE ceremony was ended, the guests were standing about chatting with each other, and Paul ran his finger around the neckband of his starched shirt, wondering how much longer the evening must go on. The English officers, resplendent in dress uniforms, talked with the parents of the bride. The orchestra of violins and flutes began to play, and the bride opened the dancing with her new husband. Half a dozen other couples joined them in a rowdy country dance.

Angélique Cuillerier was dancing with James Sterling, who was looking at her as if he thought she was beautiful, Paul observed. He watched the dancing a moment and then looked toward the corner where his father was talking with some of the French guests. Uncle Antoine was glowering at Angélique and her partner. A moment later one of her brother's friends asked her for the next figure in the dance, and James Sterling sauntered across the room to join the English officers.

Paul, bored, sneaked around to the dining-room door. Louis La Butte was there, and he made signs that he was starving. The tapers were lighted, and some of the older people, who didn't care about dancing, were gathering about the table. Paul slipped in and joined them, holding onto himself as he edged through the guests so that he wouldn't crowd in too fast and be dragged back by his mother, who was easily embarrassed. The food at these parties made up for all the bother of dressing up, and Paul felt more cheerful.

Just as he picked up a plate, someone jogged his elbow. Clutching, to keep the plate from slipping from his fingers, he looked over his shoulder.

Cousin Angélique murmured, "Paul, can you come away for a minute? I've got to talk to you." She looked around quickly and lowered her eyes again. "They're all dancing; no one will notice. Quick!"

With one hand under his elbow, she moved Paul toward the back door of the room, chatting about the pleasant night as they went. Paul grabbed a couple of pieces of bread and cheese as he left the table, and then, holding his plate before him and thinking sadly of all the goodies he had not yet collected, he accompanied Angélique through the door into the back garden. The house was so crowded and the crowd so gay that no one noticed them leaving.

The night was warm and still, and the frogs were piping loudly along the river bank. Angélique led him away from the house into the darkness at the back of the garden, and motioned him to sit down on a fallen log. He began to eat his bread and cheese. He was hungrier than he had realized, and he wished he'd picked up more food.

"Paul," his cousin said, "listen to me very carefully."

He liked his cousin. She was the prettiest girl he had ever seen. None of the women in the town could understand how she had reached her mid-twenties without being married. Lately his mother had been telling his father that Mr. Sterling seemed to be paying Angélique a lot of attention. She twisted her hands together and looked down at them.

"There is great danger, Paul," she whispered. "I don't dare talk to anyone else about it."

He sat up, flattered and alarmed.

"You know my—my friend, Mr. Sterling?" she asked. "In the fort? Next door to your store?"

"Of course." Even in the darkness, he knew she was blushing hotly.

"I'm afraid for him . . . Look, Paul. Pontiac is going to attack the fort. Tomorrow. My father is . . . well, he's with Pontiac." She spoke reluctantly. "He doesn't like Mr. Sterling, because he's English. And Alexis is with the Indians, too. They were watching me tonight, and I couldn't say a word to Mr. Sterling. I can't talk to Major Gladwin tonight, or to Captain Campbell, or to any Englishman. But you're my own cousin, and if anyone asks any questions you can say I was asking about Philippe."

She drew a quick breath, and Paul sat very still.

"I heard this plot in my father's house," she said. She sounded stubborn and defiant. "Pontiac will come to the

54

"Paul," his cousin said, *"listen to me very carefully."*

fort tomorrow with four hundred Indians. They'll carry their sawed-off guns under blankets, and every Englishman in the fort will be killed. Can you tell Major Gladwin this, before tomorrow morning?"

Listening to her, Paul forgot his hunger, letting the plate slip from his fingers into the grass. Across his mind ran thoughts of all his English friends: Captain Campbell, Billy Turnbull, John Rutherfurd, Bill and Jack in the garrison, the Girard's good neighbor, James Sterling.

"I'll tell him, Cousin Angélique."

She clutched his wrist tightly. "Paul, you mustn't tell anyone else. And you mustn't tell anyone how you learned this. If my father knew I'd done this, he'd beat me till I couldn't stand. And Alexis would beat me. I'd never see Mr. Sterling again . . ." She looked over her shoulder as if she feared listening ears in the darkness, and Paul, listening with her, shivered a little.

"My father must never know," she repeated. "Nor your father, either. I thought you'd be smart enough to figure out how to tell the major without his knowing it came from me. Can you do it that way?"

Paul felt tall and strong and competent. His cousin, ten years older than he, had turned to him when she needed help.

"What shall I tell the commandant, exactly?"

She described the plot she had overheard, and Paul nodded. "I'll tell him tonight."

"Oh, Paul, you're such a comfort!" She sighed with relief and hugged his shoulders. "So smart and strong and big for your age! Thank you a thousand times. Perhaps some day I can help you."

They made their way back to the house, and Angélique slipped, unnoticed, into the crowd in the dining room. Paul remembered he had left a plate lying on the grass in the garden and decided to leave it there. He picked up another, wondering, as he filled it with cakes, bread, sliced meat, and cheese, just how he could speak to the major in private. As he was leaving the table he looked around the room for the commandant, and saw him and Captain Campbell bidding the Navarres farewell. James Sterling was nowhere to be seen, and Angélique was flirting with a young Frenchman.

Paul looked at his filled plate and crammed a piece of meat into his mouth, trying to think of some other time, some other way, to speak to Major Gladwin. "Tomorrow morning," Angélique had said. Any other time might be too late. This was the moment. With a sigh he put down his plate and made his way through the laughing crowd to a side door, where he let himself out without seeing his hostess or his parents.

The two officers were striding along the river road toward the fort, and Paul had to run to catch up with them. Panting, he drew abreast. "Major Gladwin, sir! I have a message for you."

Major Henry Gladwin was a man in his early thirties, of moderate size, high color, and little humor. In this hostile wilderness, his responsibility was to hold this fort for England. He was conscientious and competent, and in his life there was no compromise with orders. While he lived, Detroit would be an English fort.

His second in command, Captain Donald Campbell, had taken temporary command of the fort when the French colors came down. He was a fat, friendly, near-sighted Scotsman, who spoke both the French and Indian languages, and both groups liked him. When Major Gladwin arrived to take over the fort, both French and Indians were grumbling about the Indian policy of the English, and the new commandant welcomed the captain's experience and insight. The men were fast friends.

As Paul hailed the major, both men halted. Major Gladwin looked aloof, as if he wondered why he was being chased at this time of the night. Captain Campbell smiled at the boy quizzically.

"I've learned of a plot," Paul said hurriedly. "Pontiac plans to come to the fort tomorrow morning with sixty of his chiefs and ask for council with you. All will carry sawed-off guns and tomahawks under their blankets, and three hundred of his braves and women will wait at the gate with guns and tomahawks and knives. After he has spoken in council he will offer a peace belt of wampum, green on one side and white on the other. He'll show the white side while he talks. But when he turns the green side to you, it will be the signal for attack. The chiefs will fire upon the officers, the Indians in the streets will attack the garrison. Every Englishman will be killed."

As he spoke, the import of what he was saying became real, and he began to tremble.

"Where did you hear talk like this?" Major Gladwin demanded.

He sounded as if he didn't believe a word of the story, and Paul stared at him beseechingly. It was terribly important to make the major understand the danger.

"Sir, I can't tell you that. But I heard it from someone who was present when the plan was formed, and who wanted you to be warned."

"French?"

"Yes, sir."

The major said, "Humph!" and stood there, looking away into the distance, scowling a little, as if he were trying to decide exactly what this meant. Paul looked at Captain Campbell. He had known the captain longer than the major. The captain was looking at Paul gravely, and the boy met his eyes.

"Captain Campbell, the French think the Indians are rising. I've heard that three times lately."

"And why do they think that, sonny?"

"My brother says the Indians are very angry . . . " He found it was hard to say "with the English" to English officers, and he let his voice trail away.

Captain Campbell said to the major, in a low voice,

"The boy's brother is a voyageur. He knows the Indians well."

"Ah?" Major Gladwin looked intently at Paul again. "So you think this plot is likely to succeed?" He still sounded incredulous, and Paul became impatient.

"Sir," he stood very straight, "if Pontiac enters the fort tomorrow morning with sixty chiefs, every Englishman within the walls will die. But the Indians will not touch a single Frenchman. The French have nothing to fear, and some even hope they will again hold the fort, if the English are destroyed."

Major Gladwin nodded. "I daresay. The French have been friendly in the main, but it would be impossible to believe they really like us. Thus," he glanced at the other officer, "they have nothing to gain in warning us of an attack. . . . Yesterday, Monsieur Gouin, from the coast, told me the French suspected the Indians were readying for an attack on the fort. And now this . . ."

"Monsieur Gouin has been friendly," the captain commented.

In the distance, the long-drawn-out war whoops and the Indian drums sounded. These had not been heard in two and a half years. The three looked at each other. In the moonlight Major Gladwin's face was stony. He looked at Paul again.

"This is a valuable service," he said stiffly. "We shall be prepared to resist Pontiac's attempt. In the name of the garrison, I thank you for the warning." He reached out and shook hands with Paul, and the two officers strode off together. Their pace was a little faster than before.

Paul watched them until they faded into the darkness and then turned back to the party. Perhaps now he could have some supper.

In the big room the women were sitting together, fanning themselves and gossiping, curled and powdered heads together. The younger men were dancing, and pretty girls were coquetting with them. Angélique was dancing with her brother, and she saw Paul standing on the edge of the dance floor, smiled at him, and raised her eyebrows as if to question him. He smiled back, nodded ever so slightly, and she turned gracefully in the figure of the dance, with a satisfied expression.

At the far end of the room Henri Girard and Pierre La Butte were talking with Antoine Cuillerier and half a dozen other men. Out in the dining room Louis La Butte was looking over a table stripped of its bounty. Paul started in that direction, and almost tripped Alexis, who turned in the figure of the dance and stumbled over Paul's foot. He caught himself with an ugly scowl and a muttered oath. Paul dodged away and found himself next to the men around his father.

Antoine Cuillerier was saying, "Let me remind you gentlemen that when the English leave, this fort will again be French. And I, for one, should like to see that day."

"Nonsense," Pierre La Butte told him gruffly, "when we

pledged allegiance to England over two years ago, it was bcause France was conquered everywhere in this land..."

"*Except* in Louisiana," Cuillerier interrupted. "Louisiana is not so far from here. If we overthrow the English —and with the help of the Indians that should not be hard—our French brothers in Louisiana will join their boundary with ours, and France again will hold the heart of this continent."

"Impossible!" Paul's father spoke emphatically, and all the men turned to listen. "A foolish dream! What do we care for kings? Some day the English may be gone, or they may not, but we habitants, we'll be here forever. Let us not have war, that is what I say. We've been at peace ever since the English raised their flag over Detroit, and I say, let us leave it that way."

He looked beyond the group as he spoke and saw Paul listening, his mouth open and eyes agog. Henri gestured to the men and said sharply, "What are you listening for, Paul? This is for men, not children!" With a wave of his hand he dismissed the boy, and Paul, humiliated, cheeks burning, turned as if he had heard nothing he could understand, and went on to the dining room where Louis was picking up crumbs from the table with a moist forefinger.

"Where were you all evening?" Louis asked. "This was the best party I've ever been to—best food, that is."

"I wouldn't know." Paul tried to sound lofty. "I haven't eaten yet."

Louis looked at him curiously. "Must have been something pretty important, to keep you away from food," he observed.

"I guess I wasn't very hungry." To his own surprise, Paul found this was true. One forlorn scrap of cheese lay on a blue plate. But he didn't want it after all. He wandered back to the crowd in the big room. You never knew what you might overhear if you kept your ears open.

But the party was breaking up, guests were bidding their hostess farewell, and Henri Girard called his family together. As they walked home along the dark path by the river, Paul walked with his father; his mother and Suzette followed, bringing the younger children.

Still angry and humiliated over his dismissal earlier, Paul stalked along saying nothing. He wondered if his father knew of any plot to attack the fort. If he did not, Paul was not going to tell him. He began to regain his composure a little as he thought about his dark secret.

Chapter 5

S ATURDAY morning was bright and warm. The sky was more brilliant, the south wind softer, the sun more smiling than any day since winter had begun to recede. The fort, freshly washed by yesterday's rain, was sparkling clean when Paul opened the door of his father's shop at eight in the morning. The streets were full of people talking with each other about the war drums last night, and the double sentinels at the gates today. James Sterling came over to the Girard shop.

"Are you expecting to do business today?" he inquired.

"Aren't you?" Girard asked.

Sterling raised his eyebrows humorously, as if he didn't want to seem fussy. "I don't like to seem agitated, you know, but if the Indians are going to make trouble I shall certainly lock up my store."

Girard said nothing. He was busily straightening out his shelves and placing new merchandise on view. Paul looked from his father to Mr. Sterling, wondering if he should tell them what he knew. He was about to speak when his father turned and said, "Paul, go out to the warehouse and fetch in those bolts of ribbon. With Rogation Days coming, we can sell ribbon."

When Paul returned from the warehouse, Mr. Sterling had gone back to his own store, and other English traders were collecting there. They talked in low voices, and each carried his gun. The church bell in Ste. Anne's steeple rang nine o'clock.

Paul was too restless to stay indoors. When his father wasn't looking, he slipped out to see what news he could pick up. At La Butte's house in Ste. Anne Street he found Louis standing in the door watching the uneasy activity in the streets.

"What's going to happen?" Paul asked.

Louis shrugged. "Who knows? It's said the Indians are going to attack the fort, but no one knows for certain."

"Where's your father?"

"He's gone to talk with the officers. Pontiac has asked for a council..."

Paul looked down Ste. Anne Street toward the parade ground where a hundred English soldiers were performing an exercise drill. The big gate beyond the parade ground was open, as it always was, but two sentinels each held a fixed bayonet. Beyond the gate a crowd of Indians milled about in the field.

Paul's throat was dry, his breath came quickly, and he tried to think of something he should be doing. At last he said to Louis, "Come on down to the gate," and the two boys went to stand near the sentries where they could watch the Indians through the open gate. Some of them were playing lacrosse, which they often did on that meadow. But there must be three hundred, Paul figured, and some of the braves were stalking back and forth, staring at the palisades.

Then, beyond the common, Pontiac came striding out of the forest along the river road, with a long line of chiefs marching behind him.

A hush fell over the fort as if everyone came to attention at the same moment. Paul looked back over his shoulder. The English traders were standing outside their closed doors, muskets in hand, waiting. Just waiting. The church

Pontiac thrust his chin up, as he marched up to

bell began to ring ten o'clock. And Pontiac reached the east gate.

The war chief and his sixty warriors were painted with black and white war paint and wrapped in colored strouds; and they wore the eagle plumes of war. Their eyes gleamed darkly, their mouths were stern. The sentinels made no move to stop them. Paul's heart began to pound.

Pontiac marched through the gate arrogantly, and the sentinels stood at attention as his followers passed through.

Captain Campbell's house, followed by all his men

In silence he led his warriors across the parade ground to the meeting place. Forty of the Indians in the meadow shuffled after them, clutching their blankets closely about them. Paul watched them: if he hadn't known they carried guns, he would have suspected nothing.

Pontiac saw the English garrison, and his face darkened in an angry scowl. The soldiers who had been moving in drill figures were standing stiffly at attention, each holding his bayonet at the ready. Pontiac thrust his chin up, and his steps lengthened, as he marched up to Captain Campbell's house, where the council was being held, and through the door, followed by all his men.

Paul stood still, his eyes fixed on the closed door of the house. He thought of the plot Angélique had described. The war belt—when Pontiac turned it from white to green . . . . Sixty Indians in that house faced two officers with two interpreters. How could the plot fail? And why didn't Gladwin shut them out? Why? Why? Why? The questions pounded angrily in his ears, and he felt confused and helpless.

"They look as if they wanted to fight," Louis said broodingly. "They don't look like a peace council. Let's go around and listen in."

The boys looked up and down the narrow streets. Indians had posted themselves at every shop, near the gates, and around the barracks. Every Indian in the meadow had come inside. There were three hundred in the streets, as well as the sixty warriors with Pontiac. If the chief's plot was successful, every Englishman would die. Today.

Would he be brave enough to fight with these doomed men? Paul asked himself, feeling as if he were having a nightmare.

He followed his cousin around the block and through a wooden gate that gave into the courtyard behind Captain Campbell's house. In the back wall of the house the mullioned windows were opened to the warm sunlight of the spring day, and the speech of the men within came clearly through. The boys crawled quietly across the courtyard and huddled below the windows.

Pontiac was speaking, and the Indian syllables fell harshly upon the boys' ears. Paul shuddered. Then he heard La Butte interpreting for the English.

"We are greatly surprised, brother, at this unusual step thou hast taken to have all the soldiers under arms, and that thy young chiefs are not at council as formerly. We would be very glad to know the reason for this, for we imagine some bad bird has given thee ill news of us, which we advise thee not to believe, my brother, for there are bad birds who want to stir thee up against thy brothers, the Indians, who have been always in perfect friendship with their brothers, the English."

Major Gladwin's voice sounded, answering this complaint. Then there was a long silence. Unable to endure it, Paul stood up and looked through the window, and then ducked down again.

"Nobody saw me," he whispered. "Pontiac is standing there, holding the wampum belt. He keeps fingering it and smoothing it and looking at it now and then . . ."

Pontiac was speaking again, in sad tones. "Six of our chiefs have died in the past winter. Will our brother give us something to calm our minds and banish our sorrow?"

Again there was silence. "Look again," Louis whispered.

Paul peeped over the sill. In that still room all faces were fixed upon Pontiac, who held the wampum belt as he looked at Major Gladwin. He held it white side out, he raised it as if he would hand it to the major . . .

Major Gladwin lifted his hand, and a rolling thunder of drums broke upon the silence. Paul dropped flat to the ground at the first drumbeat. When the drum roll ended he could hear Gladwin, speaking as calmly as if he were entertaining his good friends.

"We grieve with you for your chiefs, our brother. And in their memory we give you these six suits of clothes and this bread and tobacco. May they calm your minds and banish your sorrow . . ."

The boys lay still as death. The Indians were departing from the council house. They were marching out the door and into the street with measured steps. The boys sneaked out of the back gate and sauntered toward the La Butte house, trying to act as if they had been enjoying a walk in the sunshine.

Scared faces showed in every window. Frightened

women looked out, holding their babies tightly. Small children were screaming, demanding to know what the noise was. A small, rough-haired terrier was running in circles, barking in hysterical excitement.

From La Butte's house, the boys could see Pontiac marching, with a cold and furious air, across the parade ground to the east gate with his warriors. The other Indians straggled after them. The garrison stood at attention, bayonets gleaming in the sun.

The stolid sentinels watched the Indians leave. As the last one went through, they closed and barred the gate. The garrison was ordered to stand at rest.

Major Gladwin and Captain Campbell stood at the door of the captain's house with the two interpreters. The major was filling his pipe, tamping the tobacco tightly into the bowl with one finger.

"I'm surprised he didn't attack," he said, poking into the bowl of his pipe as intently as if that were the chief business of the day. "He brought more Indians inside with him than we number soldiers in our garrison."

Captain Campbell shook his head. "We've not seen the end of this yet," he said, in his thick Scottish brogue. "Pontiac had more men than we have, yes. But our soldiers were ready, and an Indian wants to win without losing a man." He laughed. "This is too sensible for the English! We're ready to die for victory! But an Indian will run away and hide rather than be killed. And then he'll come back for a surprise attack when he thinks his chances are better. . . . No, Major Gladwin, Pontiac withheld his attack today because he would have lost many men, even if he won the fort. But he'll try again, and soon. And we should close the gates and keep him out next time."

Pierre La Butte was nodding as if he agreed. Major Gladwin put the pipe into his mouth and the three men moved into the street toward the parade ground where the major dismissed the garrison.

"I know you thought I should have closed the gate in his face today," the major said to the captain. "But he would have denied any reason for such treatment, after coming and going freely all this time. And above all, Lieutenant Robertson and Sir Robert Davers are in Indian territory at this moment. If we angered Pontiac without reason, his allies might attack Lieutenant Robertson's party. . . ."

He drew a deep breath and looked very grave. "I wonder, even, if the drum roll was a mistake." He sighed. "How can you know when you're right and when you're wrong until blood has been shed? La Butte, what do you say about today's business?"

La Butte stared impassively into Major Gladwin's eyes. "I've known these Indians all my life, and there will be more to this than today's council. Pontiac will try again. Don't let yourself be surprised."

The major weighed his interpreter's words, and then he clapped the Frenchman on the shoulder. "I daresay you're right, La Butte, although I hope you're wrong. Will you be with us, if we're in trouble?"

They had reached the corner of the street, and La Butte turned to leave the officers. He smiled one of his rare, warm smiles. "Sir, I'm with you."

Both officers smiled broadly, saluted him, and walked on. Louis and Paul ran to meet the interpreter.

"Is there going to be war with the Indians?" both boys demanded.

"I'm afraid there will be."

"Will we leave the fort?" Louis asked.

His father shook his head. "I stay with my friends, and my family stays with me."

Louis looked at Paul questioningly, and he said, not meeting his cousin's stare, "I'd better get back to the store." Hastily he ran up the street.

He had no idea what he would do in a war between the Indians and the English—a war between Philippe and the English.

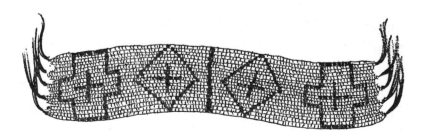

Chapter 6

WHEN the Girards went to mass at Ste. Anne's Church on Sunday morning, the fort was quiet, the fields surrounding it bloomed in sunny stillness, and not an Indian was in sight. It seemed as if yesterday's scare had been nothing but a bad dream. But the big gates were closed now and guarded by double sentinels.

The story of Pontiac's council on Saturday had swept through the fort, and opinions were divided. Some of the French openly supported the English; many said nothing at all, and Paul knew they felt as Philippe did. The English traders jested about Pontiac's plans as if the whole thing were a game.

Paul heard them, puzzled. He knew the danger in which they stood, if Pontiac overwhelmed the fort. He understood that their attitude was one of courage rather than foolish optimism. But it was a lighthearted courage that was new to him and unexpected from the English. A sense of admiration was growing slowly, and leaving him confused about his loyalties if the looming struggle broke into war.

At the dinner table Paul said, "Do you think the Indians will try to attack again, Father?"

His mother looked distressed. The twins weren't listening, but Suzette and Félice stared at him fearfully. His father said sternly, as if he should not have asked such a question, "I don't think about the Indians, Paul. Nor about the English. This is a matter that does not concern me. We're safer if we stay apart from the whole thing."

"But won't Pontiac attack the habitants, when he's overthrown the English?" Paul persisted.

M. Girard shook his head emphatically. "Pontiac is not stupid, that one! He's used to white men and their ways, their ammunition, and their gunsmiths. He doesn't want to lose them altogether. But he's discovered that the English are different from the French, and he likes the French better."

He spoke a little smugly, as if pleased to have the Indians prefer his people to the English. Then he shrugged and slapped his hand down on the table authoritatively.

"It's not our problem," he repeated. "All that concerns me is that my family shall be safe. If we keep to ourselves and take no part in this quarrel, no one will bother us."

A sound of Indian yells arose in the afternoon sunlight, and Paul rushed to the door. A band of Indians was whooping and running to the playing field across the river.

"They're going to have a game of lacrosse!" he cried. "Maybe I can play."

He ran out of the door to find Louis, and the boys left the fort by the water gate. If the Indians wanted to play lacrosse with the French, as they did on so many Sunday afternoons, they could not be planning for war. Paul felt as if a cloud had rolled away from the sun, as he and Louis pushed off in one of the canoes on the river bank, and crossed to the playing field.

Philippe was there, chatting with his cousin Alexis and a handful of his French friends. He was talking gaily, and Alexis, glancing away from the group as Paul and Louis approached, raised his hand in a quick signal to Philippe not to let his talk be overheard, and then smiled at the younger boys as if glad to see them. "Today, my young friends, you can play. We need more men for our team."

The game began with shrill whoops. It was a fast, rough game played with long, curved rackets and a small, hard knot of wood, and Paul loved it. After an hour some of the other young Frenchmen arrived, and Paul and Louis dropped out.

They went down to the river to get a drink and dip their heads in the cold water. They they recrossed the river and walked through the quiet forest, circling around behind the fort to call on the Turnbulls.

Mrs. Turnbull had placed a pan of gingerbread on the window sill to cool, and the spicy smell filled the farm-yard as the boys went up to the door. Billy was chopping wood, splitting chunks of log and throwing the pieces on a large pile beside the door. As the boys came up, he left the axe sunk in a log and cried, "Great! Just in time for Ma's gingerbread!"

They sat on the stoop before the front door looking toward the fort, waiting for the warm cake to cool, and talking about the Indian plot of the day before.

"Why don't you move into the fort?" Paul asked. "It's safer, if the Indians are restless."

Billy shook his head. "Why should they bother us? We never gave them any trouble. We're way back here. If they want to hit the fort we might be better off away from it. What's got them stirred up, anyway?"

Paul shrugged. "The English aren't giving them the presents they're used to, like powder and lead," he said; it was the first thing that came into his head, and he remembered the Indians in the store a few days ago, who were so angry about the English regulations. "Why do the English try to change things?" he asked impatiently. "We French never had any trouble with them."

Billy laughed. This was an old argument between the boys, and he refused to take it seriously. "We don't want to support these savages the rest of our lives with presents and charity. If we stop giving them powder and balls, they'll get used to paying for what they want like everyone else."

It was hard to counter this argument. All Paul could say was that this was the way it had always been. We share what we have with our friends, he thought, and they share with us . . .

At that moment an old Indian shambled across the yard and went around to the back. Paul watched him idly.

Everyone knew old Gray Wolf. He had been a chief once, it was said. But now he drank too much and begged food of everyone, too lazy to work. At Mrs. Turnbull's door he whined, "Give present?"

Mrs. Turnbull looked at the old man, at once annoyed and kindly. "Here," she thrust the pan of gingerbread at the Indian, "take this home to your squaw and her babies, and leave me alone!"

Stolidly the old man stalked away toward the forest, now and then sniffing the fragrant cake he carried. Paul watched the gingerbread go, wistfully. Just because an Indian beggar came along he would have no gingerbread today.... Billy was grinning at him.

"So you think we ought to keep handing out presents?" he teased.

Uncomfortably Paul got up. "I've got to get home," he said. Louis joined him. Billy waved and went back to his woodchopping.

As the boys went along the rough wagon road that led from the Turnbulls' farm to the fort the air quivered with Indian yells. Paul and Louis could see the sentries on the ramparts walking more quickly, watching the forests intently. The boys began to run, and as they came up to the gate, a halfhearted burst of laughter sounded from the garrison.

"False alarm!" yelled one of the soldiers. "Looks like the French boys in their boats out there are trying to raise a scare!"

But the horseplay of the young habitants suddenly revived the tension that had set in the day before. Paul was more frightened for the Turnbulls than they were for themselves, and angry that they would not move to the fort. And yet, as Billy had said, would they be any safer inside the walls? Not if the Indians determined to attack in force.

Monday, the ninth of May, was a Rogation Day, one of the three holy days preceding Ascension Day on Thursday, and all the habitants in the community attended mass at Ste. Anne's. They followed their pastor in a chanting procession to bless the fields outside the walls, and the fields and meadows were empty and quiet. On the walls the soldiers were preparing the cannon for fire, and making ready for defense against surprise attack.

Back in the church, Paul's mother whispered to her neighbor, "There are no more than a hundred and fifty English, counting traders as well as soldiers. And Pontiac has four hundred braves!"

"My husband says the commandant has no provisions for war," her neighbor whispered back. "He heard there is hardly flour enough for two weeks—and almost no pork! The spring shipment has not yet come from Niagara. And now the Indians will surely capture it before it reaches Detroit."

"T-t-t-t-t," Mme. Girard clucked. "But what can one do?"

They shook their heads together and turned their attention to the celebration of the mass. After church the Girards walked home in silence. Nobody felt like talking, and Paul, trying not to think about choosing between the English and the Indians, was almost too melancholy to eat his dinner.

After dinner his father went out to consult with his brother-in-law La Butte, and Paul accompanied him. When Louis said, "Let's go down to the willow grove," both fathers were talking too busily to be interrupted, and the boys slipped out and left the fort.

The river glimmered tranquilly in the sunlight, violets and buttercups were thick along the river path, and the forest was full of bird calls. The boys climbed into the willow trees and hid where the leaves were thickest. For an hour they talked about many things: their Indian friends; Philippe; their English friends; the adventures they would have when they were Philippe's age; the Rutherfurd party that should, by now, be well on their way up Lake Huron.

Suddenly Paul stiffened. "Look!" He pointed to the river.

A dozen Indian canoes filled with braves were speeding toward the fort. Pontiac sat in the first one, his face cold and determined. The boys stared at each other, and then, without a word, shrank into the foliage of the tree until they were invisible. In silence they watched the Indians beach their canoes near the meadow outside the east gate and form in a line behind Pontiac as he strode up to the gate.

Pontiac pounded on the great gate, which swung open. Two armed sentries faced him. He talked to them, and they shook their heads, muskets crossed. Pontiac's head lifted arrogantly, and he thrust out his dark face, demanding entrance. The sentries barred the way with stolid determination. Then, with an exclamation that carried to the boys a quarter mile down the river, Pontiac turned abruptly and signed to his braves to leave.

Cold and menacing, they stalked away from the gate, following their chiefs to the canoes. Watching them, Paul swallowed. In spite of his father's assurance that the Indians would not touch a Frenchman, he felt as if a murky danger hung directly over him. The canoes sped past like angry wasps, toward the Ottawa encampment, where the campfires sent quiet smoke spirals into the still air.

They're going to attack, Paul thought, and it was hard to breathe. *They're going to attack the fort any minute. And the garrison is so small...*

He sat very still. Louis said, "Maybe we'd better go back."

Quickly and quietly the boys slipped down the tree, watching for hostile eyes as they went. As they reached the path, running feet and Indian yells sounded somewhere ahead of them. They stopped where they were, ducking behind the nearest trees.

From where the boys stood, they could see the meadow

before the east gate of the fort. A band of thirty savages, brown and shining in the sun, their faces gleaming with war paint, were running across the meadow yelping like dogs on the heels of a hare.

"They're going to the Turnbulls!" Paul said breathlessly.

"Isn't that Otussa?" Louis demanded. Paul looked at the running gang. It was Otussa, and he felt sick.

Forgetting caution, the boys ran down the path and across the meadow at top speed. They pounded and yelled at the gate, and it seemed like an hour before the sentry opened it.

"The Indians are going to the Turnbulls!" Paul cried. "Can't you do something? Quick! Quick!"

Even as he spoke, the death halloo sounded. With a sob, Paul ran to the nearest ladder and climbed up to the north rampart, where he could see the Turnbull farm. Louis was at his heels, and as he stood beside Paul on the rampart, the second death halloo sounded. And the third.

"That was their scalp yell," Jack Bradshaw said to Tom Smith, looking grim. "Means they've spilled blood."

The two boys stared at the farmhouse, shaken and sick. Paul could not look at Louis. They knew what the death halloo meant. The Indians had killed Billy, their good friend. And Billy's brother. And his mother, who had given gingerbread to an Indian only yesterday. Paul began to tremble, and he clung to the palisades, so he wouldn't pitch off the high walk. His friend Otussa had done this.

With a sob, Paul climbed up to the north rampart

"I'm going to tell my father," Louis muttered, swallowing hard. No one said anything, and he slipped down the ladder. Paul was staring through wet eyes at the Turnbull home, paying no attention to his cousin's departure.

Flames shot up from the roof of the Turnbull house, and the Indians streamed out of the door and began to drive oxen and cows into the pine woods back of the farm. They tomahawked a stubborn ox that refused to move, and the cow that stood stubbornly by her calf, and left the carcasses on the ground amid the squawking hens. A barking dog stood his ground until they disappeared, and then sat and howled his own requiem for his dead masters.

"The Turnbulls were my friends," Paul said, feeling that someone ought to know. His voice came out shakily. Jack Bradshaw looked at him and then stared over the ramparts again. "I guess you'll have a chance to get even. They're asking for a fight."

Tom Smith cocked his gun and fired it into the air to test it. Paul was trying to hold back tears, and swallowing many times to ease a hurting throat. A hatred for the Indians boiled up, and he nursed it angrily.

He was looking down river when a canoe full of Chippewas pulled up at the water gate, let a Frenchman out at the landing place, and sped upstream. Paul scrambled down to the ground and ran to the water gate. He knew that man.

The Frenchman stumbled, exhausted, through the gate,

and asked hoarsely for the commandant. Then he moved shakily across the fort, supported by a couple of soldiers, to Major Gladwin's house.

When the soldiers came out of the house, Paul asked, "What happened to Lieutenant Robertson's expedition?"

"Did you know the Frenchman?" The soldiers stopped. "That's Monsieur Desnoyers, one of our customers. We sent flour to him with the bateau. What happened?"

"The Chippewas attacked the bateau last Friday. They killed Lieutenant Robertson and Sir Robert Davers, and a couple of sailors."

"What about John Rutherfurd?" Paul was afraid to hear.

"Indians took him away with some of the soldiers for slaves. Desnoyers saw Rutherfurd a minute before the Indians took him."

"Does he know where John is now?"

"Desnoyers thinks the Chippewas are adopting him. Those Chips that brought Desnoyers here—they're joining Pontiac."

Paul heard him, as if from a great distance.

"You all right, kid?" the taller soldier asked him.

Paul shook his head and cleared his eyes with his fists. He knew now which side he would be fighting on.

"I'm all right. It's my friends I worry about..."

One soldier looked at the other, and both patted Paul on the shoulder. "You'll feel better when you fight, boy. It works that way."

Chapter 7

THE night was quiet, but the dark horror that had fallen upon the English settlers overhung the fort. Paul lay on his bed in the loft of the little white house on St. Joseph Street, feeling the weight of the silence, and thinking, thinking.

He must do something, and carrying a gun on the sentry walk was not enough. A hot surge of rage flooded through him, and he beat the bed with hard fists, swearing that he would exact revenge from the Indians for the Turnbull massacre. But the rage passed, and he knew that vengeance was not enough either. The Indians had taken John Rutherfurd, too, and when he thought about that Paul shuddered.

Then he sat up, holding his head and praying to the Virgin to give him strength. If he could go to the Indian camp where John was held prisoner, perhaps he could save him. If he could find Philippe in the Ottawa camp, perhaps he could save all the English. Then he lay down again, beaten and discouraged. How could anyone stop the gathering thousands of Indians from killing all the English?

As the darkness lightened into the early gray dawn,

long-drawn yells and war whoops shattered the silence, and a clamor of bullets struck the stockade from all sides. Paul lay very still, his hands tightly over his eyes, and groaned. In those early hours when courage runs low, and fears are overwhelming, he was sure the Indians would overrun the stockade and he would witness the horrible deaths of all his friends. For himself he feared nothing. Pontiac had said no Frenchman would be touched. But he would be safe only if he stood aside and made no move to help his friends.

He sprang up from the bed and made his way downstairs, where his family was gathering for breakfast. The racket of bullets was incessant.

His mother was cooking his favorite pancakes. She looked sad and stern. Suzette was knitting on a stocking, pale and unhappy. Félice was playing with the kittens on the floor. The twins came in from feeding the chickens. Mme. Girard set a plate of hot cakes before her husband, who sprinkled them with brown sugar.

"What will happen today?" she demanded. "We should lock the store, if the Indians are going to take the fort."

Henri Girard shook his head. "They won't take it today. Major Gladwin was wise not to let them in yesterday."

"Philippe—" Paul's voice was trembling, and he stopped. No one said anything. His father looked anxious and angry. His mother's eyes filled with tears, and she turned away.

The attack went on into mid-morning, until the twins were edgy and complaining of the noise. Paul's father went to confer with Uncle Pierre La Butte, and Paul went down to the barracks to find out from the garrison how the fight was going.

Five men had been hit and lay where they had fallen, some unconscious, two of them moaning heavily. Captain Campbell was directing their removal to Ste. Anne's Church, which the priest had offered as a hospital. He looked up as Paul approached.

"You can help us with these wounded, my boy," he said, getting up from his knees heavily. "I fear we've lost more than the enemy, and we can ill afford it."

Paul helped carry the wounded into the church, and there he made them as comfortable as he could, bathing their faces, finding pillows for their heads, covering them with blankets, and bringing cold water to drink. When the doctor arrived, Paul went on to La Butte's house to find his cousin. The firing had died away, the yelling slackened, and the day quieted.

"My father's gone out to talk to Pontiac," Louis reported. "Your father went with him. Major Gladwin said he thought Father could persuade the Indians to settle their demands peacefully."

"I wish there was something we could do," Paul said restlessly.

"There's nothing now until Father gets back."

Paul was very tired, and he realized suddenly that he

had not slept at all during the night. The day was quiet now, with a warm, muggy blanket of air smelling of powder settling over the fort. He went slowly up the sloping street, past the church where he could hear one of the men still moaning, and back to his home, where he fell on his bed and went to sleep.

When he awoke, it was late in the afternoon. He stretched, listening to the pleasant homely sounds of cooking in the kitchen. A wooden spoon was beating a pudding, someone was whisking egg whites into a froth. In the courtyard the children were shrieking at the antics of the kittens. Somewhere a dog was barking furiously. For a moment it seemed as if peace had returned. Then he remembered his father's errand, and he jumped up and went down to the kitchen.

"Has Father returned? What happened at the council?"

"He has just left with Uncle Pierre," his mother said, not looking up. She was mixing a soufflé, and she gave it all her attention. "Pontiac wants Captain Campbell to come to his camp and talk about a peace treaty."

"Does Father think this is wise?"

"Monsieur Gouin was there, and three other men from the coasts. They all felt Captain Campbell should talk with Pontiac, that anything should be done that might please the Indians and stop this cruel war . . ."

Paul went to the door. From there he could see a crowd gathering around the east gate, and he ran down to join them.

Captain Campbell and Lieutenant McDougall were jesting with Pierre La Butte and Henri Girard, as the sentries stood back from the open gate to allow them to go out. Four Indian chiefs awaited them, and a large crowd of Frenchmen followed the officers, chattering and laughing. Paul fell in with the crowd.

"What do you think will happen at this meeting?" he asked M. Césire, an elderly man trudging along in a blacksmith's apron and *sabots*. M. Césire stared at him as if wondering what he meant.

"Captain Campbell is so upright a gentleman that Pontiac must respond to an officer like him, who is willing to go to him and discuss a negotiation like this."

"Will Captain Campbell be safe, do you think?"

The man's eyes filled with horror. "But of course! Who could wish him harm? Pontiac has asked for him because the captain has been a friend of the Indians these many years, as he has also been our friend." He looked at the crowd of Frenchmen about him. "When this trouble is ended, we'll all be free to go about our affairs again. Until then, it's a bad business, is it not?"

Paul nodded and moved on through the crowd, to listen to the talk of the others. They all felt as the blacksmith did, that Captain Campbell could bring about an end to the fighting. One man was saying as Paul came up, "Monsieur Gouin sent word that this was a trap, and the captain must not go. Do you know what our captain said? He said, 'Who is fearful for me, if I fear nothing meself?'

and then he said, 'I offered to talk to these Indians. A Campbell has given his word, and a Campbell keeps it.' He is truly a man of courage, is he not?"

"Truly a man of courage," Paul agreed.

They were meeting Pontiac in Antoine Cuillerier's house, a half mile from the fort, and as they approached, the braves awaiting them split the air with menacing yells. Pontiac, smiling at the loyalty of his men, came forward, greeted the two officers, and led them inside the house. The habitants followed, and Paul wedged himself inside the door among the last.

Antoine Cuillerier sat in the middle of his big living room in a velvet coat, keeping his laced hat on like a king. He watched the English officers approach him without rising. The Indian braves ranged themselves about the walls of the room in a restless circle. Henri Girard stood back with the other habitants in one corner. Pierre La Butte stood beside Captain Campbell and Lieutenant McDougall. The crowd of habitants was silent and watchful.

Pontiac stepped forward and addressed Cuillerier as "Commandant of Fort Detroit." Paul stared from one to the other. Cuillerier looked complacent, as if he liked the title. Captain Campbell stared at Pontiac in angry astonishment, and Pontiac turned to him confidently.

"We offer peace, Captain Campbell. Your officers and men will lay down their arms, give up their luggage, and leave the fort with empty hands. And we shall escort them safely to Fort Niagara."

The fat Scotsman was silent for a moment. Lieutenant McDougall looked ironic, as if he had expected nothing less, as the interpreter gave Pontiac's offer to the officers in English. Then the captain said with dignity, "I understand your terms, Chief Pontiac. But I must talk with Major Gladwin before I can give you an answer."

"Will you return John Rutherfurd to us?" the lieutenant asked. Paul leaned forward to hear the answer.

Pontiac's face seemed to close up. "I know nothing of him."

After a few more minutes of discussion, the captain turned to the lieutcnant. "We might as well return to the fort," he said. He was calm and unruffled as always, but Paul sensed an undercurrent of anxiety. To Pontiac the captain said, "What if our commandant refuses your terms?"

Antoine Cuillerier sat in the middle of his big living room in a velvet coat, keeping his laced hat on like a king

Pontiac pulled back his lips in a savage grin. "Then the war will continue, and thousands of my allies will join me."

"We've heard your terms. Now we'll take them to Major Gladwin."

Pontiac looked at his braves, and six of them stepped forward, surrounding the two officers. Silence fell upon the crowd, as the Frenchmen looked at one another, realizing that Pontiac had trapped them all into believing his good faith. Two of them looked at Pontiac defiantly, and the blacksmith said firmly, "Captain Campbell, you are free to return to the fort whenever you wish."

The Indian chief looked from the blacksmith to the captain to the habitants, measuring them with his eyes. "When Captain Campbell and Lieutenant McDougall have slept in my lodges for two nights, we will send them back to the fort."

The silence was thick and dark. Frenchman looked at Frenchman, eyes dropped under Pontiac's stare. Feet shuffled. And Cuillerier looked around the group, bold as an eagle.

"Do you fear your friends, Pontiac's people?" he challenged. None answered. "You need not be alarmed, Captain Campbell," he said in a cold tone. "Pontiac will see that you sleep safely."

Captain Campbell met Pontiac's eyes and shrugged. "I fear nothing, my friend. Perhaps when we've spent two nights together, our friendship will be stronger."

Lieutenant McDougall was pale. But he stood as firmly as his chief, his head high, his back straight as a steel rod. Pontiac waved to the habitants to depart. And slowly, slowly, the French settlers who had accompanied the officers so confidently turned and went out the door. The last to leave were Pierre La Butte and Henri Girard.

Paul waited for them and fell into step beside them. The three walked toward the fort in silence for some minutes. Then La Butte sighed and spoke slowly as if a weight depressed him.

"Now, indeed, I fear we should have listened to the warning of Monsieur Gouin," he said to his brother-in-law. "I fear for these good men."

Girard was staring toward the stockade, his mouth set angrily.

"I, too, believed Pontiac was negotiating in good faith," he said. "Now I do not know what to believe."

He looked as if he felt the same shock of betrayal that had struck Paul when the Turnbulls died.

Chapter 8

THE ugly muttering buzzed through the English garrison whenever a Frenchman appeared near the barracks. On Wednesday night Paul went to see his friend Jack Bradshaw, and as he approached the barracks someone yelled, "Where's our captain, Frenchie? What did you give him to Pontiac for?"

Paul went into the barracks and found Jack polishing his gun.

"Hello there." Jack sounded neutral. But Paul felt a coolness.

"I wish you English could realize that the French feel betrayed too!" he burst out.

Jack glanced at him. "Why? Pontiac didn't keep one of your men."

"But he said 'two nights' and Captain Campbell and the lieutenant said they would stay. Surely Pontiac wouldn't betray a flag of truce! He *must* return the officers."

"Looks to me like you don't know the Indians as well as you're supposed to," Jack said bitterly.

That made Paul feel like a fool, and that was even worse than feeling misunderstood. "Could I fight with the garrison if I got a gun?"

Jack shrugged. "Why not? We can use a few more men . . . " He glanced at the boy as if he were a stranger. "Maybe."

As unhappy as if he, personally, had delivered the English officers into Indian hands, Paul left the barracks and walked slowly back home. It looked as if the English didn't want him fighting with them.

He had never before cared what the English thought of the French. He had thought only of his feeling for the English. He had begun to like them when he became friendly with Jack and Tom in the garrison, and the liking had grown with his friendship for Billy and John. He had begun to admire them when he had seen Major Gladwin facing Pontiac in the council, last Saturday, and the admiration had deepened when he had watched Captain Campbell go out to meet Pontiac.

He couldn't bear to be thought a traitor to the English command. Brooding and melancholy, he walked around the fort. There must be some way he could prove his loyalty. Rounding the corner where the arsenal stood, he found Major Gladwin studying the wooden building gloomily, with his aide.

"If they begin sending burning arrows, we're lost. All these wooden buildings will go up at once."

"Yes, sir." The aide agreed with his chief.

"Something I can do, sir?" Paul saluted the commandant. At least Major Gladwin knew of his loyalty. The major looked at the boy as if he were surprised to see him.

"Oh, Paul! Yes, you can do something. Go through the fort and get the citizens to set out tubs and barrels and fill them with water. Tell them to keep them filled until the war is over. We must be ready to put out any fires if they get started, and I can't spare a man from the firing lines."

Paul darted away to call on every Frenchman. All of them realized the danger of the Indians setting fire to the fort, and agreed to set out the buckets of water. Paul walked through the fort again, checking the preparations, and reported back to the major.

But there must be something more important he could do. More than anything he wanted to be a hero. He dreamed about that ambition the rest of the night. But how could he do something heroic, cooped up inside the fort?

On Thursday the firing was incessant again, and more men were wounded. The noise died away toward evening, and Paul roamed restlessly about talking to the settlers. He found small comfort there: some of the French were determinedly neutral, some were hoping for an English defeat. Disconsolately he went to find Louis, and the two went over to stand near the barracks, hoping there would be some way to convince the garrison they were friendly to them. The officers of the garrison were entering Major Gladwin's house in a body.

"Going to talk about the situation," one English soldier said, gesturing toward the officers with his thumb.

"They got two choices," said the other. "Surrender or fight. If you ask me, a lot of the officers would like to surrender. They'd just as soon go back to Niagara, where they ain't got so much trouble with the Injuns."

If the English gave up the fort, Paul thought, Antoine Cuillerier would be the commandant, and the Detroit territory would be French again. He'd rather have the English.

"Well, we ain't got provisions," the first soldier said gloomily. "From the looks of it, those Injuns could overrun the stockade any time they'd a mind to. On the other hand," he brightened, "I heered the boats was coming down from Niagara with gunpowder and food—and some more men. They oughta be along any day now ... "

"The major ain't one to knuckle down to an Injun like Pontiac," his companion remarked, shaking his head in admiration. "He's stubborn. He'll keep this fort, I'll lay you odds."

"He won't even talk terms till he gets his officers back."

"Aw, no Injun ever stayed at a fight more than a couple of days," the first said disdainfully. "Any Englishman can outstay any Injun two and three to one." He noticed the boys standing nearby, and said with annoyance, "What do you want? Beat it!"

Flushed and angry, the boys walked on. Sometimes the English irritated Paul deeply. And yet he wanted them to like him. He glanced at Louis. The La Buttes were under even darker suspicion than the Girards. Soldiers said openly that Pierre La Butte had betrayed their officers to the Indian chief. Louis felt even worse about this shadow of hate than Paul did, and Paul could think of nothing to say to him.

He left his cousin and climbed the sloping street to his home. He was going to show them all, Paul thought. He dreamed of the gallant courage that would relieve the garrison, subdue the Indians, and cause Major Gladwin to pin a gold medal on him before all the assembled troops, telling them that without Paul Girard all the English would have been slaughtered.

The way to find the opening for all this accomplishment eluded him. He went to bed feeling that life was blocking him in every direction.

The days went by on heavy feet. The English officers remained in captivity, and by Sunday there was no doubt that Pontiac had violated his own flag of truce, and his invitation to the officers to visit him in order to negotiate terms. Henri Girard hardly spoke to his family when they returned from church and sat down to the midday dinner. After he had eaten he said brusquely, "I go to have council with my brother La Butte," and he left the house again.

"Your father is very angry," Marie Girard said to the children. "The Indian chief has affronted his honor, and this is very bitter for a man like your father. Robert, go to the pump and fetch us more water. Charles, look to the cow ..."

Paul sat at the table when the twins had left, leaning his head on his hand and thinking. His father was angry because the English despised him and the rest of the French. If Philippe had stayed at home it would have helped. But Philippe was out in the forest with the Ottawas . . . Out there one could do great things. Paul sprang to his feet. If he could talk to Philippe . . .

He ran out of the house and through the streets to the commandant's house. The young aide who answered his knock looked very supercilious.

"The major is very busy," he said. "Captain Campbell is in the hands of the Indians, as you probably know."

Paul felt that the aide was blaming him personally. But he thrust his chin up and spoke doggedly. "I know. That's what I want to talk to Major Gladwin about. I have an idea that might help."

The aide looked so scornful that Paul knew he was about to dismiss him without further delay. But Major Gladwin himself walked across the hall just then and caught Paul's last words.

"Oh, Paul, it's you," he said, approaching the door. "So you have a plan for our captain, do you?" He said to the aide, "This is the boy who warned me last Friday of Pontiac's plot to murder the garrison. He's worth listening to . . ."

The aide stepped back, an unwilling respect showing through his stiff manner, and Major Gladwin told Paul to continue.

"Sir," Paul said, "my brother lives with the Ottawas. I'd like to go to the Ottawa camp and talk to him. I might be able to discover more of Pontiac's plan for this war. And I could ask Philippe if he knew of any plan for releasing the officers..."

The commandant looked at the boy thoughtfully. "You speak the Ottawa tongue?"

"Well enough."

The major nodded. "By all means, go ahead, Paul. If you can discover any means of escape for Captain Campbell and Lieutenant McDougall, we shall reward you handsomely. We value our officers highly and ... " He hesitated ... "Captain Campbell is my good friend. If you can inform us of the Indians' numbers and munitions, this will be useful."

"Thank you, sir." Paul saluted.

"How long will you be away from the fort?"

"I don't know how long it will take, sir. But I'll return as soon as I have something to tell you."

"Good enough." Major Gladwin sat down at a small table in the hall and scribbled a note. "This will admit you to the fort again, Paul, if there's any question. We haven't closed the gates against Frenchmen yet—but that may come."

Climbing back up the sloping street from the major's house, Paul thought about his plan.

The Ottawas had moved their encampment on the first

day of the war to the north side of the river where they had pitched their tepees on the farm of Baptiste Meloche, two miles from the fort and near a small stream called Parent's Creek. Baptiste Meloche was a friend of Philippe's, and Paul knew him well. He grimaced at the thought. Like Alexis Cuillerier, Baptiste openly supported Pontiac's war.

Paul left the fort at night when he could move across the open land and through the forests with greater safety. His mother had wrung her hands and wept when he said he was going to join Philippe in the forest. His father had stormed about his being foolish, too rash to use good sense, rebellious against his parents, and no better than his brother. But in the end, when Paul produced the major's permit to leave the fort and re-enter, and persuaded them to listen long enough to understand that he was going on an assignment for the commandant himself, they calmed down and conceded that, while they did not like his taking such responsibility upon himself, he must go.

"But take care," his mother said over and over. "Do not stay away too long. Do not take foolish chances. What if the Indians decide they hate all white men, and kill you as they did the Turnbulls?"

Paul shrugged off her fears. But underneath he knew they were justified. The Indians might turn against the French at any time. He hoped he might be able to accomplish this errand without arousing any suspicions.

But that problem he was not going to think about until he had to.

He made himself a packet of meat and cheese and bread; he slung a rolled blanket around one shoulder; he kissed his mother goodbye; then he walked to the gate with his father. The sentry let him out of the gate, and he looked back to wave to his father. Henri Girard was standing in the light of a lantern, and it seemed to the boy that his father looked old and tired. Suddenly he wanted to turn back.

He hesitated a moment, then resolutely walked toward the river bank and along the river to the Meloche farm. In the daytime Paul knew this footpath as well as the floor of his own house; in the darkness it was different. He had to move more slowly to avoid rustling the leafy branches that overhung the narrow path; he had to feel his way carefully to keep from tripping over treacherous roots. But after the first half hour the moon was high, his eyes had accustomed themselves to the darkness, and he could move more quickly.

He crossed the footbridge at Parent's Creek and passed the Meloche house. There was candlelight in the windows. He moved closer to the house and looked in. Inside the living room four men were talking: Baptiste Meloche, Philippe, Captain Campbell, and Lieutenant McDougall. The English officers were in full uniform, as they had been on Tuesday.

Paul hid in the thick shrubbery at the side of the house,

Henri Girard was standing in the light of a lantern.
Suddenly, Paul wanted to turn back

waiting for Philippe to leave. It was late, and the moon was low again, when Philippe came out. He stood at the door with his host and talked quietly with him for some minutes. Then he swung into the lane and walked with quick, silent steps toward the Indian tepees—at least a hundred of them—that were scattered through the trees beyond the house.

Paul followed his brother closely, until he entered a tepee. Paul crept up and stood outside the tepee for several minutes, wondering if Philippe was alone in there. Then, as no sound issued from the tepee, he laid his ear to an opening in one of the seams of the fabric and listened intently. He could hear the breathing of only one person. He lifted the flap, entered, and let the flap fall behind him.

Standing there in pitch blackness, he listened again to his brother's breathing, uncertain whether he was awake or asleep. And then, as quietly as a falling leaf, he heard Philippe say in the Ottawa tongue, "What do you want?"

Paul dropped to his knees, feeling lightly with his hands, and whispered, "Philippe, it's Paul."

Philippe sat up with a start, and Paul found his hand in the darkness and grasped it. "Paul, what do you want here?"

Suddenly Paul was too tired to hold his eyes open. "Tonight I want only to sleep. Tomorrow we must talk."

Philippe pulled Paul down near him on the ground. Paul rolled up in his blanket and fell asleep almost before his brother had turned over.

Chapter 9

WITH the early rays of the sun, the Indian encampment came to life. Dogs barked and snarled, women began grinding corn, a couple of babies cried and then were still again. Cookfires blazed before the tepees, and slim blue curls of smoke rose in the still air. A great, blue heron rose up from the river on slowly flapping wings, jays screamed at each other in the forest, a cardinal called for its mate.

Philippe stretched and rolled over. Paul sat up and looked at his brother, pulling his blanket about his shoulders. The early morning was cold, but the smell of the forest was fresh and wild. Philippe rose a little and leaned on his elbow.

"What are you doing here?" he asked, keeping his voice low.

"Did you know the Indians killed the Turnbulls?"

Philippe lay back on the ground again, staring at the smoke hole in the top of the tepee. "I knew."

"Were you with them?" Paul had to know.

Philippe shook his head. "No. I hate the English, but I wouldn't kill an old woman and a couple of boys who were farming."

Paul drew a deep breath of the chill air and felt better. "Did you hear about John Rutherfurd?"

"I heard. He's all right. His master is very fond of him."

"Where is he?"

"Miles from here. With the Chippewas."

"Where is that village?" Paul asked.

His brother looked at him shrewdly. "You think you can rescue him?"

"I'd like to get him away, yes. You know yourself the Indians are flighty as the wind. They could turn upon him . . ."

"You'd better leave things alone," Philippe said. "You could do more harm than good." Then, as Paul's jaw hardened and his eyes darkened, his brother said, "The Chippewas will be joining Pontiac some time soon." He looked at Paul curiously. "What are you here for?" he asked again.

"Can I stay with you awhile?"

"As you like." Philippe spoke warningly. "Don't expect to spy on the Indians and go back to the fort. They know you're my brother, and I won't have you betray me. If you want to go back to the fort now, you can go. But by tomorrow you can't leave."

Paul sat silent for several minutes, thinking.

"I'll stay. I could do nothing for the English or the French, either, inside the fort. I was cooped up, it was intolerable. Out here in the forest I can breathe again . . ."

"You may be more like me than I had supposed." His

brother smiled, half sardonic, half pleased. He sat up and threw back his blanket, stretching and rubbing his arms and legs in the cold air. Then he sprang up and put on Indian dress.

"I'll tell my friends you've run away from the fort," he said. "But I'll tell you this: if you try to run back again, you'll be shot. The Indians will let no Frenchman carry information about Pontiac's plans."

Paul stood up and stretched, too, not meeting his brother's eyes.

"I'm staying here."

The next days went by pleasantly enough. The Indians did not question the presence of Philippe's brother, and Paul was kept busy finding food for Philippe and himself. The Indians, who never laid in stocks of reserve food, could rely now only on what they could find in the forests from day to day, and what they could take from the settlers along the coasts. Between days of firing upon the fort, warriors and braves called on the habitants to demand food and ammunition. Much of the time they hunted and fished.

One day, as Paul was grinding dried corn for Philippe, Otussa passed the tepee with a rabbit snare.

"So you have joined us!" he said, looking pleased.

"I wanted to see Philippe." Paul remembered Billy Turnbull, and wished now he had not seen Otussa. He turned back to his task, hating himself, and the Indian came to

As Paul was grinding corn, Otussa came and stood before him

stand in front of him. Paul looked up angrily. "Why do you kill the English?" he cried.

Otussa's face darkened. "They take our land, they spoil our hunting, they treat us like slaves. The French are our friends, but the English—no."

"You were with the braves who killed the Turnbulls," Paul muttered, accusingly, grinding the corn more rapidly, and not looking up.

"I am an Indian," Otussa said, looking very proud. "I must earn the right to be a brave. Some day I must be a chief, and for this I must prove myself. Yes, I went with that hunting party. The Turnbulls were no friends of ours."

"But they never hurt you."

"They were English. They took our hunting land for farming."

"Some Indians are friends with the English."

Paul looked up then and was startled. Otussa's jaw was set like stone, his mouth was tight, his eyes gleamed like dark fire.

"Some, yes!" he spat out. "Some who would betray their own people, some who can live with the white men. But not I! I am an Indian like my forefathers. And I can never live with the English."

"And yet a friend of mine is living with the Chippewas now," Paul said. "The Englishman, John Rutherfurd. His master treats him like a son."

The Indian shrugged indifferently. "Some of our people

like to keep a captive Englishman. Then he lives as we do."

"If you see John Rutherfurd, will you treat him as a friend of mine?"

Otussa stared at Paul intently. Then he nodded. "Your friend will be safe with me."

The corn was ground, and Paul stood up, stretching tired and cramped muscles. "It's been long since we raced," he said, wanting to move about. Without warning he set off for the river. Halfway to the goal Otussa drew abreast of him and reached the shore ten steps ahead. Both boys flung themselves down upon the sandy margin, breathing deeply. Otussa was smiling. And Paul felt torn between his anger at the senseless murder of his English friend and his affection for his Indian friend. He could understand Otussa, and, understanding, he could not hate him.

He would not think about the war while he was with the Indians, Paul told himself. He would try to forget it until he returned to the fort with the information Major Gladwin wanted. So he hunted, fished, raced, and wrestled with Otussa, loving the active life in the forest. Some days he heard the war whoops and the firing on the stockade. But the attacks were neither so long nor so concentrated as those he had seen from within the walls, and he paid little attention to them.

This was a good life, and he had missed it since the

war had begun. But even as he wrestled and competed with Otussa, struggling intently to outdo him, Paul was aware for the first time of a difference in his Indian friend. There was none of the lighthearted gaiety he knew with his French friends or his English comrades. Otussa spoke often and intensely of the need to win glory. And Paul, who had very little ambition, who lived from day to day, carefree and reasonably content, found this burning ambition uncomfortable. True, he wanted to do something heroic for the English garrison under siege. But he did not dwell on this hope very often. Otussa's ambition touched everything he did, and he never allowed himself to betray either anger or great pleasure.

This was new, Paul thought. Last summer when he had spent much time with the Indian, Otussa was more open, easier to understand; he had laughed more. Now he was a year older, he had reached the age when youths trained for manhood, and he was training himself with rigid determination. Paul admired his discipline. But more and more he felt Otussa's hostility toward the white men, and it made him uneasy with this long-time friend.

When he had been with the Indians a week, a band of Chippewas arrived and Paul went with the Ottawas to greet them. The Ottawas whooped and cheered as ten war canoes filled with Chippewas lined up along the bank of the Detroit River. Chief Sehakos stepped from the first canoe and saluted Pontiac.

"Welcome, my brother Sehakos," Pontiac greeted him. "We rejoice that you join our war upon the English. How many braves do you bring?"

"We bring one hundred and twenty braves to our brothers," the Chippewa chief replied. "The Master of Life inspires us to war, as he inspired our brothers, the Ottawas."

Seizing tomahawks, the braves of both bands danced in celebration, shouting and singing the war chants. Paul watched them closely.

Suddenly, for some unexplained reason, his attention was drawn to a man in the last canoe. The man was brown, he wore a breech clout, and his head was shaved, except for a small tuft of hair upon the crown and two locks, braided with silver ornaments, hanging over his face. He was painted like the other warriors, but something in his manner was different. He glanced around as the others exchanged vows of loyalty, and when all other eyes were fixed upon Pontiac in dark, gleaming excitement, this man looked beyond the Indians toward Paul. His blue eyes lighted with recognition. Paul found himself tightening so suddenly that for a moment his head swam. It was John Rutherfurd, dressed and painted like an Indian.

Pontiac addressed the assembly, smiling proudly at the numbers of his warriors. The *Michigan* had sailed from Fort Detroit that morning, he told them, and was now moored at the entrance to Lake Erie. This must mean she was waiting to escort the boats from Fort Niagara that would bring reinforcements for the garrison. While she was anchored there, Pontiac's forces would attack her. The braves cheered.

Furthermore, Pontiac went on, there were now so many Indian warriors allied with him that many could be dispatched along the waterways to intercept the reinforcements. Cheering again, the braves began to brag of taking Fort Detroit and the reinforcements, as well as the *Michigan*. "The *Michigan* has a crew of only seven men," Pontiac told his cheering braves. "We can send out four hundred, and she is ours!"

Paul listened, deeply uneasy. The danger to Fort Detroit was great. But even if he could manage to escape his brother's vigilance, what could he tell Major Gladwin? Only that Pontiac had gained many reinforcements, and planned attacks that the garrison would be helpless to counter. There was no way to warn the oncoming boats, no way to help the *Michigan*, moored miles from the fort, in Indian territory.

The council was over, and the Chippewas moved away from the river bank to set up their tepees. Rutherfurd's master led his family to a spot not far from the Meloche house, where they set about building a bark house. The Indian squaw and her two children seemed to regard John as one of the family. He moved freely about, without ropes or manacles, and Paul was interested in the way the young Englishman had adapted himself to Indian ways. But he dared not approach Rutherfurd openly.

The next morning Philippe told Paul he was going up the river with some of Pontiac's braves to look for the bateaux from Niagara. He kept watching Paul as he talked. "You will stay here today. Pontiac wants no spies with him."

Paul looked up. "I'm planning to stay. Don't worry..."

Philippe smiled confidently. "Of course you're planning to stay. Pontiac's young sons and their dogs can watch you as well as I can—and now that the Englishman has come to our village you will have company."

In the encampment the women were setting kettles on the fires to boil fish and soup, and pounding the dried corn for the day's meals. Through the trees Paul could see some of them digging in small cleared areas and planting the corn for this summer's crop. Back of the bark house John was setting out corn for his mistress. She was working at the far end of the row, watching her captive suspiciously. Paul watched, hidden in the trees. When the mistress left the cornfield for a moment, he whistled very softly. The English boy stood still, then stooped to plant four more grains, looking over his shoulder toward the trees. Then he saw Paul, and his face lighted in the old smile Paul remembered.

Paul came forward a little, and John left the field and

joined him. "My brother is living with the Ottawas," Paul told him. "I left the fort ten days ago. I hoped I could find you! Are you well, John? How are you treated?"

"They treat me well," John said. "Peewash is very fond of me. He talks of adopting me! Quite an experience, I daresay, being adopted into an Indian tribe!"

"But do you like the Indian life?"

The youth shrugged. "It was rough, getting used to it. I was sick for some days. But now I'm as hard as any Indian, and I must say I feel very good. I hope . . ." He stopped and looked cautiously around before he continued in a whisper, "I hope I can escape some day. But they watch me all the time. And I know now that an Indian can track a man through these woods almost faster than he can run. I used to talk about escaping with some of the soldiers that were taken with me. But we never found a way that would be practicable."

"Perhaps you and I can form a plan," Paul whispered.

A footfall sounded somewhere near him. "I'll come again tomorrow," Paul said quickly. Rutherfurd picked up some wood and moved on into the forest without another word. Paul moved noiselessly toward his own tepee.

Now he was in no hurry to return to the fort. He had achieved his own most important objective: he knew John Rutherfurd was alive and well, and within shouting distance of the fort.

There was no chance to see John the next day. It rained

such torrents that even the Indians stayed inside their tepees. Not a shot sounded that day. And in Philippe's
tepee, rivulets of water ran across the grassy floor.

The day after that Paul watched the bark house for
hours, from a hiding place in the forest. Peewash was
constantly at John's side. Paul saw them go off together to
hunt, and, later, go into the Meloche house. He wondered
if John had a chance to talk to the English officers quar-
tered there.

At the close of the third day, just as the sun was sinking,
a wild yell of triumph sounded through the camp from
the river, and Paul and Philippe dashed over to the shore,
to see what had happened. Three Indian canoes filled
with Hurons had beached upon the river's edge. One of
them flew a captive red flag of St. George, and its party
was waiting to disembark.

As Paul came up, a hundred Indian warriors, Ottawas
and Hurons, lined up in a double row with spears, tomahawks, and clubs in hand, yelling ferociously. A British
officer, the only captive, stepped from the canoe with the
red flag and faced them coolly. Paul watched, his heart
pounding. Beside him, Philippe's face hardened cynically.

The officer began running between the lines, trying to
shield his head from the blows that rained upon him. He
staggered under the force of the clubs, dragged himself
to his feet again, and stumbled on. Paul felt his breath
coming quick and hard. If the man fell he was lost. And
even if he reached the end of the gauntlet, he might be

beaten to death there. It was a long run, and the screaming was almost worse than the beating. Blood streamed from cuts on the officer's head, his uniform was torn and smeared, he reeled and almost fell. But with superhuman effort he dragged himself ten more steps to the end of the line. Paul shut his eyes. He didn't want to see the end.

A female yell made him open his eyes again. A middle-aged squaw was claiming the officer for her second husband, defying the warriors to take him from her. She was holding him up, and he looked as if he had fainted.

Philippe murmured to Paul, half cynical, half admiring, "That's Ensign Pauli, the commandant of Fort Sandusky. Only one left of his garrison."

"When did this happen?"

"Ten days ago. The braves were talking about it."

The officer raised his head and pulled himself upright. The squaw explained to him in guttural Indian syllables that she had saved his life and he was now to be her husband. His face twisted in pain, but it might have been from the beating. Resolutely, in sign language, the Englishman expressed his appreciation to her for having saved his life. Then he limped away with her.

Paul watched him go, uncertain whether to feel glad or sorry for him.

Chapter 10

THE news of the fall of Sandusky was important, Paul knew. But Philippe was watching him more closely than ever, and he must betray no idea of returning to the fort. Planning ways to escape, Paul fell asleep. Perhaps the next day . . .

But in the morning Philippe shook him awake, impatient to be up and leaving with the Indians. "Pontiac is going to take the *Michigan* this morning," he told Paul, his eyes alight with excitement. "You will go with us. He'll take all his braves down to the Potawatomi camp and attack from there. This may end the war!"

Paul had no choice. He accompanied his brother in a canoe that carried three Indian braves, and he saw with dismay that Captain Campbell was in Pontiac's canoe.

"Pontiac is taking Captain Campbell along so he can order the sloop's captain to surrender," Philippe told Paul, smiling at the brilliance of this strategy.

"Captain Campbell won't do it!" Paul cried, looking at the straight, plump back of the Scottish officer in the canoe ahead.

Philippe laughed at him. "Of course he will! Pontiac will be holding a gun behind him. Do you think your captain will find it worthwhile to die for nothing?"

"He'd die rather than take orders from Pontiac," Paul declared. "Pontiac has behaved like a traitor, holding the officers and dishonoring the flag of truce!"

Philippe scowled, looking remarkably like an Indian.

"Pontiac has more sense than all the English officers put together," he cried. "He wants to drive the English off his land. He wants to get rid of them without losing his own men. Why should he fight by English rules? He fights like an Indian. He's no traitor, he's a brilliant military leader who makes his own rules."

"You sound like an Indian," Paul accused him.

Philippe looked at him levelly. "I feel like an Indian. I want the land free to hunt, free of men who would cut down the trees and drive away the game and the wilderness. Why should we let the English fill up our land? We French hunted it as the Indians do. But the English— they overrun everything, they take over everything, who can live with them?"

Paul said no more. Silently the brothers paddled past the fort where the guards on the stockade stared stolidly at the canoes passing by, and made no sign.

The *Michigan* had been standing guard at the mouth of Lake Erie for five days now, waiting to escort the bateaux from Fort Niagara that would bring the badly needed men, food, and munitions to Fort Detroit. As the Indians approached the ship, the crew of seven men lined up with Captain Newman along the side of the vessel.

Fifty canoes filled the water, each carrying eight to ten Indians yelling defiance. The Indians began to brag among themselves how easy it would be to take a ship with only seven men in it. The brothers' canoe was in the circle back of Pontiac's canoe, and Paul could hear the chief clearly.

"When we are close to the English ship you will order her captain to surrender to us," he told Captain Campbell.

The captain stared at Pontiac, his nearsighted eyes unwavering. "That I'd never do, Great Chief. You can put me to death first."

Pontiac scowled, and turned toward the sloop.

"We have here your captain, Englishmen!" he cried in Ottawa language to the men hanging over the rail of the sloop. "He will tell you to surrender. If you do not, he will die." The men at the rail looked at him soberly, understanding his intention, though not his words.

Captain Campbell waved his hands to the captain for attention. "Ahoy! Captain Newman!" he cried.

Pontiac, understanding no English, sat back and watched him, smiling.

"Disregard this Indian chief," Captain Campbell ordered. "In the name of our commandant, Major Gladwin, I order you to do your duty as you see it."

The captain smiled broadly; then turned and gave quick orders to his men. They scattered from the rail, the sails began to fill, and before the eyes of the astounded Indians, the vessel sailed away from them. One or two canoes gave chase. But shots from the ship's guns struck the water close enough to splash them, and they gave up the chase and turned back. Pontiac kept looking at Captain Campbell, angry but puzzled, as if undecided what to do to him. In the end the canoes went back upstream to the encampment.

"Disregard this Indian chief," Captain Campbell ordered

Philippe was silent for many minutes. Paul said nothing, thinking about the captain's courage. At last Philippe said, "He is a brave man, your captain."

"Very brave."

"This will make the war last longer."

"The English will never give up."

"Then they will all die. After all, Pontiac has a thousand Indians now, and more will join him."

Paul said no more. He was so filled with admiration at the quiet courage he had witnessed, that he wanted only to think about it. An Indian was reckoned brave when he fought to kill and gain glory for himself. He proved his bravery when he withstood tortures without a grimace. But—Paul's mind was going off in a direction it had never taken before—he had never admired the heroism of the Indians the way he admired Captain Campbell this morning, and he wondered why that was.

Suddenly it came to him: an Indian must be brave and strong to win glory for himself and gain leadership. But Captain Campbell had performed a brave action for the sake of his fellows, the garrison of Fort Detroit. He would have sacrificed himself without a second thought. Paul contemplated this kind of courage all the way back to the Indian village. Before this summer Philippe had been his hero. Philippe had killed a bear with his own hands. But could Philippe be as brave as Captain Campbell? Paul wondered.

More than ever, he wanted to get back to the fort. But

Philippe was watching him closely, and Paul could not even get away to look for John Rutherfurd. A couple of days after the *Michigan* had sailed, Philippe took Paul with a hunting party to look for food.

Though the party of eight ranged for miles, they found only a few careless rabbits. At the end of the day, Otussa, who had been hunting for his father, walked home beside Paul, who was discouraged and hungry. He had shot nothing. Otussa had two rabbits, and he gave one to Paul. "This will make you and Philippe a good supper."

He was generous, Paul thought, accepting the rabbit gratefully. The Indians were always generous with their friends. He was tired and thoughtful. They walked along in silence.

An Indian from another tribe joined the group, and began talking in low tones with one of the warriors. Paul heard him clearly, but he betrayed no understanding.

"The Englishman left Niagara twelve days ago," the Indian spy was saying. "Tell your chief he brings ninety-six men and a hundred and thirty-six barrels of provisions."

A trickle of cold sweat ran down Paul's face, and he wiped his face with a grubby hand as if he were swiping at flies. He *must* get back to the fort, and soon, with this news!

The next morning he said to his brother, as they ate their breakfast of cornmeal, "I should like to visit Uncle

Antoine, Philippe. He might know something of our family, and I've been gone a long time."

Philippe looked at him suspiciously. But Uncle Antoine was a loyal supporter of Pontiac's war. And he was a shrewd old man, not likely to let the prize Pontiac had promised him slip from his fingers carelessly.

"Why not? We can go together. I, myself, have not seen our uncle for many days."

It was a bright, warm day, with a soft breeze stirring the forest trees, and the brothers walked at a leisurely pace through the forest to the beaten path that led past the Meloche house and southwest along the river bank to the Cuillerier house, a mile or so closer to the fort. Peewash's bark house looked deserted, as Paul watched it for some sign of John Rutherfurd.

"Peewash took his family away some days ago," Philippe said carelessly. Paul said nothing as they continued.

When they entered the Cuillerier house in mid-morning they found a couple of Indian slaves cleaning and sweeping. "Where is the commandant, Monsieur Cuillerier?" Philippe asked in the Indian tongue.

Paul felt that his throat would close up before he could call his uncle "Commandant," but he said nothing. He looked around the house with interest. He had been here before, of course, but seldom, because of his father's dislike for his rich brother-in-law.

The Cuillerier house was much larger than the Girards'. Indeed it was known in the settlement to be a rich and luxurious dwelling, and many Frenchmen envied it. The main room was a great hall in which Pontiac frequently held council with as many as two hundred braves. On one side was a heavily carved chair as big as a throne. This was the place where Uncle Antoine had sat with his hat on, the day Captain Campbell had gone to the Indian council to talk with Pontiac.

The Indian slave girl looked at them stolidly. "He's in the garden."

The brothers went through the hall leading from the front door to the back, and looked into the garden. Cuillerier was sitting in the sun, his bald head shining, talking with Alexis. Near them Angélique sat working at fine embroidery.

"We come to pay a call on our uncle," Philippe said, with a courteous bow. Paul came forward, bowed, but not so low as Philippe, and suffered his uncle to kiss him on both cheeks. Alexis welcomed his cousins with a sharp glance at Philippe, a questioning scowl at Paul.

"And Angélique, have you nothing to say to your cousins after all these weeks?" Uncle Antoine cried.

She set down her needlework and came forward, warning Paul with an uneasy glance to say nothing of the secret between them. Uncle Antoine sat down again on the grass, puffing on an Indian pipe and looking well content with the world. Philippe sat down to talk to Alexis, and Paul stared at his cousin's needlework curiously.

After a few minutes Alexis said to Philippe, "Walk back here with me. I have something to talk to you about." He rose and moved away from the group. Philippe hesitated, looking at Paul and at his uncle. Uncle Antoine stretched out on the grass, prepared to stay where he was. Philippe shrugged as if he felt sure Paul would be guarded, and followed his cousin.

A moment later Angélique said, "You must be hungry after the days in camp, Paul. Come in the kitchen and we'll order lunch for all of us."

Her father closed his eyes contentedly, as the two cousins rose and strolled toward the house. As soon as they reached the door Angélique said in a low voice, "You never told anyone except Major Gladwin of the plot I told you about at the wedding, did you?"

"Never. And now I have other news. You remember John Rutherfurd?"

"Ah, yes, poor boy!" She looked distressed. "Mr. Sterling is so concerned for him. Do you know of him?"

Paul told her of seeing John in the Indian encampment. "He was well and not unhappy," he said. "But now his master has taken him away again. If he should ever return—if his master would sell him—would Uncle Antoine buy him out of slavery . . .?"

"But of course!" she said. She laughed. "My father will do anything for me—even to rescuing an Englishman! And I would do that for James Sterling."

They were in the kitchen, and Paul stood near the little window that looked toward the clearing back of the garden. Philippe was deep in conversation with Alexis.

"I left the fort a little over two weeks ago," Paul said to his cousin in a whisper. "I wanted to find out about John, and to get any information that would help Major Gladwin. Philippe has kept such close guard over me that I cannot return."

Angélique said swiftly, "If you slip away through the front door there, they won't see you go. Do you think you could escape with so much of a start?"

"Easily!" He was in the hallway in one bound, and then he stopped. "But you—will you not suffer for this?"

Paul took to his heels

"Not I!" She threw up her head proudly. "No one has told me to hold you captive, and if Philippe is angry—well, I can talk faster than he can!"

Paul took to his heels. As he reached the edge of the forest he heard a halloo behind him, and he ran faster. Then he was out in the open meadow before the stockade, and breathing hard. He felt as if he could hardly keep going. One of the sentries was yelling at the man at the gate: "Open up! An Indian fugitive is coming!"

Paul glanced over his shoulder. Someone was giving chase, although he could not be sure it was Philippe. He heard a musket shot from the walls, and the thud of a bullet some inches behind him. And then the gate swung open, he stumbled through, and it closed behind him. Safe at last, he sank upon the hard ground.

Chapter 11

"WELL, look who's here," he heard the sentry saying. "We thought you was gone for good!"

Paul looked up at him, but the sun was in his eyes and he closed them and rolled over. Sitting up, he felt a little dizzy, but he said, "I must see Major Gladwin right away. I have some news for him."

"Right away!" The sentry hallooed to someone crossing the parade ground. "Here," he said, "this kid says he's got news for the major. Take him over there, will you? And it better be good. We need good news for a change."

"You escaped from the Indians?" the soldier asked curiously. Paul nodded. He was unsteady and he needed to think about keeping his balance. He stopped at the well at the intersection. "I need a drink of water."

The water revived him remarkably. He splashed some over his head, pushed his hair out of his eyes, stood straight, and looked at the soldier accompanying him. He was a young recruit of Paul's own age, and he was regarding Paul with great interest.

"You got friends among the Indians?" he asked.

Paul shrugged. "We've been friends for years," he said, with a strangely mixed feeling of defending the

Indians and disliking the English—even this blond, inexperienced boy who was asking questions. Then he remembered Captain Campbell, and things slipped into place again.

"Here you are," the blond boy said, leaving Paul at the door of the major's house.

Paul knocked, and the major's aide appeared. He looked surprised, and then he said, more politely than he had ever spoken to Paul, "The major will see you right away."

"So you bring us some news," Major Gladwin said.

Paul felt good. The major and all of his men were so obviously in need of some cheering word, and he could give it to them.

"An Indian brought news to the camp yesterday," he said. "The reinforcements sailed from Niagara on May thirteenth. Ninety-six men and a hundred and thirty-six barrels of provisions."

The major looked at him keenly, relief in his eyes.

"They must come soon, then," he said. "Certainly the *Michigan* will escort the boats through Indian attacks." He got up and paced back and forth across the room. "Do you know anything of the *Michigan*?"

Paul told him of Pontiac's attempt to take the ship, of Captain Campbell's action, and of the ship's escape. "And Captain Campbell? Is he still safe?"

"I guess Pontiac had to admire his courage. We went back to the village, and the captain is still safe."

"Then the *Michigan must* meet the reinforcements . . ."

"Yes, sir." The very urgency in the major's tone wakened a fear in the boy that the ship might not find the detachment.

"Has Pontiac received reinforcements?"

"Chief Sehakos brought a hundred and twenty braves. Wasson said he was bringing two hundred and fifty Chippewas. Ninivois had a hundred and fifty Potawatomies, Také brought fifty Hurons." He counted in his head, staring at the ceiling. "That makes about eight hundred braves out there, with Pontiac's own men."

The major nodded as if he, too, had been figuring to himself. Paul told him about Fort Sandusky.

"I couldn't get away before," he said apologetically. "My brother was trying to hold me in camp. At Sandusky, the Indians asked for council, and Ensign Pauli let seven of them in. One of them raised his head as a signal, and two braves grabbed Pauli and tied him up. When they carried him out, every one of the garrison—fifteen men—was killed. He was the only survivor."

He said no more. The major looked sober and thoughtful. Sandusky had fallen to a plot like the one Pontiac had planned for Detroit. The commandant slumped a little, as if he were very tired.

"By the way, we're still worried about the fire arrows," the commandant remarked. "Tell the people to keep the water tubs ready."

"I'll do that." Paul nodded. "But Pontiac won't burn

the fort and its stocks of goods unless he has to— He'd rather get the traders' goods than lose them."

"You've done well, Paul," the major said. "Thank you. You'd better go home, now. I think your family will want to see you."

Paul saluted and went out, feeling pleased with himself. He sauntered through the narrow streets, noticing changes since he had left a couple of weeks ago. There was none of the gaiety he was used to. Some Frenchmen who were gathered in front of his Uncle Pierre La Butte's store talked in low tones with gloomy expressions. A few small children played with a ball, but they seemed listless and fretful.

When he came into his own home, Félice was crying, and his mother was sweeping as if she were trying to vent her anger with her broom. When she saw Paul, she flung the broom from her and embraced her son.

"How we've missed you, Paul! And did you see Philippe? Why didn't he come with you?"

"He can't leave the Indians. He'll stay there for awhile yet. But he's well, he sends his love," he invented fluently, knowing what would please his mother. "What is there to eat? There is almost no food in the Indian village, and I'm starving."

His mother threw up her hands angrily. "Here, too, we're hungry! That English major has sent his commission to take all the surplus food from us! We, who were thrifty and foresighted, we must give our food to feed the soldiers! Ah, Paul, you cannot know how dreary this war has become. If it could only be over!"

"We all wish it could be over," he said, and he went into the kitchen to see what he could find. A leg of roasted chicken was in the food safe, and a small crust of bread. Gnawing on the chicken, he went back to his mother.

"The reinforcements are on the way from Niagara," he said, to cheer her up. "They should be here soon. And then the war should end almost any day."

"So they say," his mother said with a bitter expression, "but day after day goes by, and still we are closed up in here with less and less food. They don't even ring the church bells now, and the day is empty without them."

Paul went out to the warehouse to look for his father, and found him checking his food stocks. They were very low.

"The major's commission is going to come around and take some more in a week or so," Henri Girard prophesied gloomily. "We have barely enough for ourselves, and they take and take . . . Waste it, that's all they do. Give it to the people that never had enough sense to save up for their own needs . . ." He shook his head like a man caught in a trap. "Can't eat it up, we'll need it later. Can't save it, they'll take it. And Cuillerier out there— friend of the Indians! He just sits on money and tons of food, and has no worries."

"The Indians are taking food from everyone outside," Paul told him. "They take more than the English do."

Henri Girard brightened a little, glancing at his son from the corner of his eyes with a shrewd smile. "Ah, so that's how it is outside? Well, war is hard on everyone. If the English reinforcements just get through, perhaps we can end the war soon . . ."

On Monday morning, the thirtieth of May, the long awaited word came. At nine o'clock the sentinel in the southeast blockhouse cried, "Boats, ahoy! Boats approaching the fort, flying the British flag!"

The fort came alive, the word spread like a fresh wind. Habitants poured out of the little houses, soldiers ran from the barracks, traders closed their doors, and all collected at the water gate to welcome the convoy.

Paul forced his way through the onlookers, running to the

Paul and Louis La Butte were ahead of the crowd to welcome the convoy, and they contrived to climb up on a heavy bastion that had been built around the dock only a few days before. It was almost as high as the stockade itself, and from that spot the boys could look down the river at the boats that were sailing into the sun, their oars flashing wet in the sunlight. Paul announced to the impatient crowd, "There are many boats, a line of them. Six, I think, or seven. No, eight!!"

"Aw, why don't you tell us the British navy is coming?" one of the men shouted roughly. "How do you know they're English boats?"

"The English flag is flying from the first one."

Paul scrambled down from the bastion and forced his

water's edge. Major Gladwin stood at the gate

way through the onlookers, running to reach the water's edge. Major Gladwin stood at the gate to greet the convoy from Fort Niagara. The major was smiling as if he had expected this event right along, and was now able to get on with his duty. A color guard stood with the red flag of England behind him.

As the boats approached, the garrison broke into cheers. A cannon boomed in welcome. And the boats swerved a little, out of line, to move away from the shore and into the middle of the river. It could be seen, then, that English soldiers, guarded by three or four Indians, were rowing each boat.

A deathly silence fell upon the watching crowd. The silence was broken by the Indian war whoop of victory, coming from the boats. The first boat insolently moved close enough for the Indian victors to jeer at the horrified garrison.

Suddenly the boat turned toward the schooner *Huron*. "Fire at these beggars!" yelled one of the Englishmen. "Give us some help!"

The cannon boomed, the grapeshot rattled about the boat, and the Indians, terrified, leaped into the water. One of them clutched the Englishman nearest him, and dragged him under water. The other three Englishmen beat off the Indians with heavy blows of the oars, and a great gasp went up from the watching crowd.

The three soldiers turned the boat toward the shore and pulled it in to the sand with superhuman effort.

138

The Indians in the water, yelling spitefully, dared not approach. A cheer from the ramparts wavered and died, and a dozen soldiers hastened to pull the boat up on the sand and help the Englishmen to climb out. The Indians in the other barges forced their captives to row more quickly away from the fort and on up the river, even under the guns of the schooner.

The three who had escaped stumbled heavily up the bank to the gate of the fort.

"What happened?" screamed a disappointed Frenchman. "How did you lose the boats?"

One of the men shook his head, as if he could not think straight. Another straightened up and gestured to the soldier supporting him to wait a minute.

"The Indians attacked us back there at Point Pelee," he said, breathing hard. "We had ninety-six men and a woman and child . . ." The women in the crowd groaned. "Ten boats. Injuns ran out of the woods when we made camp, musta been hundreds of them. Killed a lot of the men right off. The rest panicked and ran. Lieutenant Cuyler got away with thirty-five men and two barges. Don't know where he is now. Injuns got all the rest . . ."

He stopped as if he was too tired to say more and staggered on to the barracks. The crowd followed, chattering with horror. And Paul, watching Major Gladwin, saw his face go white as stone, as this news of a serious defeat sank in.

Chapter 12

HEAT weighed down upon the fort, and swarms of mosquitoes surged up from the waterways and swamps to invade the stockade. The men made feeble jokes about them.

"Lucky these bugs ain't Injuns or we'd all be dead," Jack Bradshaw said, scratching the mosquito bites. "If I was a settler in this here wilderness, I'd give it back to the Injuns so quick they'd wonder what was wrong with it."

Unused to the heat, the men were sluggish and irritable. Paul fretted, too, cooped up inside the fort where the sun fell hotly upon the buildings and narrow streets.

On the fourth of June a Frenchman brought word to the fort that Fort Miamis had fallen. Ten days later Major Gladwin learned that Fort St. Joseph had been overcome. On the eighteenth of June the Jesuit priest of the Ottawa mission near Michilimackinac arrived to report that Fort Michilimackinac had been surprised and taken by the Indians. Fort Augustus had been abandoned by its garrison at the same time. The people of Detroit were stunned.

"That means Detroit is the last fort left on the Great

Lakes," one man said incredulously. "How can we last?"

"If the Indians could overrun all those forts, won't they take this one as easily?" cried one of the women.

A rough voyageur next to her said, half in jest, shifting from one moccasin-shod foot to the other. "Why not? Must be a thousand Indians out there right now, and how many we got in here? Less'n two hundred, counting every man, woman, and child, and some of them ain't worth counting."

She slapped him in a fit of terrified ill temper, and burst into tears, as she clutched her three children about her. "Can't someone *do* something?" she wailed. "Why don't the English fight?"

"You can't fight spooks and mist!" James Sterling snapped at her. Ordinarily he was the easiest and least anxious of men. Now he was edgy like everyone else. "Those savages run out of the forest like ghosts and run back in again. The men can't shoot them when they aren't there." He shrugged his shoulders and tried to resume the easygoing tone he usually spoke in. "If they aren't there they can't run over the walls." He laughed as if he had made a joke, and the mother sobbed and turned with her children to stumble down toward their house near the river wall.

Two days later they learned that three other forts had fallen: the Senecas had overwhelmed Presqu'Isle, Le Boeuf, and Venango, and had slaughtered the garrisons.

Major Gladwin stared at the man icily

"Three forts on the communication line with Niagara in one week!" one of the young English officers cried. He sounded as if his nerve was cracking. "How long can we last at this rate?"

Major Gladwin stared at the man icily.

"This fort will not fall though we are the last outpost in the entire lakes region," he said with slow emphasis, so the whole crowd could hear and understand him. "England did not send me out here to be terrified or outwitted by savages. Detroit will resist until the last man is dead."

The young officer stiffened and saluted. The soldiers, listening, straightened their shoulders and lifted their chins again. The sentinels on the ramparts stared at the threatening forests with guns cocked. And Paul again felt a thrill of admiration for the English courage.

On the twenty-first of June a loyal habitant came across the river to tell the commandant that settlers down the river had seen the *Michigan*. This was the first word of the ship since she had failed to meet the Cuyler detachment almost a month before, and relief flew around the fort like sunlight. Habitants who had quarreled yesterday spoke in friendly tones today. The *Michigan* would bring soldiers and food, they told each other, and the war would be over. They never spoke of the fate of the Cuyler detachment, but the memory hung like a dark cloud over their effort to be cheerful.

For the next two days the garrison watched for the *Michigan*. As the days went by with no word from her their spirits fell and rose and fell again. When they felt optimistic they talked about the reinforcements that would end the war the next day. When they were pessimistic, they expected to die in this fort, if not by Indian hands, then through starvation.

Even to Paul, who had lived in and loved the forest all his life, the wilderness was threatening. Now when he stood on the ramparts and watched the forest wall beyond the meadow, he was looking for attacking Indians. When he watched for the *Michigan* to appear on the river, curving beautifully through walls of trees, he remembered that death waited behind those trees.

After some days Pierre La Butte went outside to see what he could discover. He returned with ominous news: the *Michigan* was becalmed near Turkey Island, seven miles downstream from the fort, at the narrowest point of the river. The Indians were fortifying the island with trees and branches, and planned to attack the ship in force.

"Hundreds of them will attack," the interpreter reported, impassively.

The habitants gave up hope and talked in gloomy voices of the loss of the *Michigan*. A man of sense and reason would know it was impossible to hold the fort, they told each other. Without the wind, the ship was helpless; she must sit becalmed and the Indians would take her easily. Without her cargo they would all die of starvation in this fort. It was only sensible for the English to leave the fort to the French and the Indians, and set sail for Niagara.

But the wind rose a couple of days later, and at last, a week after she had been sighted at Turkey Island, the *Michigan* came to anchor alongside the *Huron,* on the thirtieth of June. The gates were flung open, and the welcoming crowd surged out to greet the long awaited men.

Captain Newman was smiling broadly as he came from the ship in the dinghy to meet Major Gladwin.

He climbed out upon the sand and saluted the major. Other dinghys followed, filled with soldiers.

"I thought you'd never get back," the major said, smiling as he glanced at the small boats landing. It struck Paul that the major smiled very little these days. "Did you meet any hostile Indians?"

The ship's captain laughed. "A week ago, back there at Turkey Island, they thought they could take us. I kept the men below decks, and the blasted savages thought we had only a dozen men aboard. They came out in canoes to board us, maybe thirty or forty canoes, and we let them close in and then we opened up: cannon, muskets, the whole ship was alight! They ran for their lives!" He laughed again. "We counted fourteen killed and as many wounded. After that they let us alone."

"How many men do you bring us, Captain Newman?"

"Lieutenant Cuyler and fifty-five men."

"Cuyler!"

The young lieutenant looked worn and hard, as he saluted Major Gladwin. "As you know, sir, I had to return to Niagara after that Indian attack on my detachment in May. Up to that time we had no idea the Indians were rising. When the *Michigan* brought us the news of your situation I was glad to return with the help you asked for."

"This is a very bad business, Lieutenant," Major Gladwin said soberly. "Very bad. But this may be the end for

Pontiac. Now that we have reinforcements, his game is up, but I don't know how soon he will know it."

He turned with the young officer to enter the fort, and the soldiers followed in a double line, heads up, chins drawn in, buttons polished, uniforms and red coats immaculate. These were men who had seen their comrades slaughtered and scalped only a month ago. They looked businesslike, determined, and, most of all, enduring.

Watching them, Paul was beginning to achieve a new understanding. Courage was not the dramatic, public heroism he had once dreamed about. Rather, he knew now, seeing the survivors of the Point Pelee massacre return to Detroit to fight again, that courage meant endurance, and heroism meant fortitude and mostly patience. It was an attitude that he had seen the men in the garrison developing and strengthening gradually as the days went by. They complained, they fretted about mosquitoes and hot weather, and sometimes they talked about the stupidity of their officers, and of the French. But never did they talk of quitting the fort or the war.

He was thinking about this new idea as he worked in his father's warehouse the next day. There was little enough to do there, but he wanted to be alone.

He opened boxes of hose and looked at them as if he had never seen them before, shook out blankets and folded them again. He handled the half dozen muskets that were left in stock, trying them to his shoulder, cocking them, pulling the triggers. They were good muskets.

He had never before paid enough attention to distinguish between different makes and qualities in any line of his father's stock. Now he remembered something Father Bocquet had tried to tell him in the lessons that had stopped when the war began. The father had said, "Some day you will want to know something of your father's business. You will need to read and write, it will be important to speak on paper in a cultivated manner."

Paul had ignored the good father and laughed to himself, telling himself that adults always talked that way, but, he, Paul, who was doing the growing up, knew better what he was going to do with his life than even a wise man like Father Bocquet.

Had he believed that only six weeks ago? He felt as if he had grown years in those weeks. He had always assured the priest that he was going to be a voyageur like Philippe. His brother could neither read nor write, and yet, look at the excellence of his accomplishment in the trade he had chosen. Why, then, should Paul study, only to throw away everything he learned, when he went into the forest to live with the Indians?

Now, for the first time, he thought that he might not live with the Indians. Perhaps, even as the father had told him, he would grow tired of living like a savage, would want to trade, to learn, to travel.

147

Thoughtfully he replaced the blankets and muskets on the shelves and looked about the great warehouse. Then he went into the house and climbed up to the loft to find the lesson books he had thrown in a corner weeks ago.

An hour later he heard the door open and footsteps as quiet as those of an Indian crossed the floor. Paul put down his book and listened at the top of the stair. Philippe had come home.

His mother was embracing him, and Paul came warily down the steps, wondering how Philippe would act toward him since his escape a month ago. But the Indians had won many victories since that day, and Philippe was smiling.

"I've missed you since you ran away," he told Paul, showing the affection he had always felt for his younger brother. And Paul was so relieved that nothing else mattered—not hunger, war, nor siege.

"But why are you home?" he asked. "Are you leaving the Ottawas?"

Philippe shook his head. His mother came in with a bowl of soup and some of her famous bread and set it before him. While he ate she sat opposite him, watching him lovingly.

"I'd like to see my family move out of the fort," Philippe said as he dipped a crust into the soup. His mother's face lighted.

"Oh, how I'd love to live outside! We've been inside the walls so long!"

"But why should we move out?" Paul demanded. "The Indians have been bothering the habitants on the coasts. We're better off inside."

Philippe shook his head and looked at him warningly. "The Indians are going to take the fort any time now." He sopped up the last drops of soup with a bit of bread. "When they do, they'll kill everyone in the fort, even the French. I wanted to warn you, Mother. I want my family to be safe."

Paul heard him uneasily. Philippe knew something, he was plotting something, and a cold hand closed about Paul's heart.

"What makes you think the Indians will break into the fort, if they have not tried it up to now? You know the Indians will never risk so many lives..."

Philippe did not meet his eyes. "Pontiac is growing weary of this war," he said. "He's going to finish it as quickly as possible, even if he must lose a man or so."

Suzette clasped her hands together and leaned toward him. "Do you know where John Rutherfurd is now?"

Philippe smiled at his pretty sister. "He's in the Ottawa camp, well and contented."

"Did Peewash return?" Paul cried.

"A couple of weeks ago."

"But will you help him escape?" she begged.

Philippe's face seemed to darken, and his eyes avoided hers. "When the time is right I'll help him. But it would be fatal at this time. At least he's safe while he stays with Peewash."

He got up and strode about the little house restlessly, as if already he felt enclosed.

"Well!" Philippe turned to his mother and sister brightly, "I've got business to do. I must call on Césire as soon as I can."

The blacksmith had his shop two blocks away, and it was reasonable enough that Philippe wanted some work done on his gun while he could find a gunsmith.

"I'll go with you," Paul said.

Philippe halted. "On the other hand, this may be the wrong time to see Césire. I need only to have the sight on the gun straightened and reforged." The explanation sounded forced. "I'm going to call on a—a friend." He winked at Paul as if to say, "I'm going to see a girl, don't tag along."

Paul shrugged. "Very well. How long will you stay with us?"

Philippe flung out expressive hands. "As long as need be. If my family won't leave the fort, I must stay with them at least for some time. So long now. I'll be back soon enough."

He flung out of the door as if it were too small for him, and strode up the narrow planked street, whistling a voyageur tune. James Sterling hailed him from his

150

shop door, and Philippe stopped to tell him about John Rutherfurd.

Paul watched him, deeply uneasy. He was sure that Philippe had not returned to the fort only to look after his family.

Chapter 13

B Y the time Philippe had been home for a day and a night, Paul began to think that his suspicions had been unjust. Philippe spent much time in the warehouse looking at his father's goods and talking about the furs he would bring him next spring. He walked around the fort chatting with old friends, with his old charm, and one and all spoke to Mme. Girard about how glad they were to see Philippe at home again.

On the second of July, the day after Philippe's return, Paul went down to see his friends in the garrison. Jack Bradshaw was cleaning and oiling his gun. Jack had been a captive of the Indians once, and he held a special grudge against them. It was comforting for Paul to talk with him about John Rutherfurd and his chances for escape.

"Did you hear Lieutenant McDougall got away?" Jack asked. "He came in this morning with a couple of traders."

"Good news! What about Captain Campbell?"

Jack shook his head soberly. "He figured he was too heavy on his feet, and if he slowed them down the whole party mighta been caught and tomahawked . . ."

"I'd like to see him back in the fort," Paul said. "I hope he can get away soon."

"So do all of us." Jack squinted along the sights of his gun. "But I don't know, now. Back east, sometimes if one captive got away they'd kill the other one." He lowered the musket and shook his head dubiously. "I don't think Captain Campbell is going to come back."

Paul was chilled. To cheer himself up, he said, "Oh, I think he'll be all right. Maybe Pontiac's keeping him to exchange when we get one of their big chiefs."

"Ha! When's that going to be? We can't get close enough to shoot an Indian, let alone capture one. If I ever get next to one, I'll scalp him."

Paul got up to leave. "Want me to stand watch tonight?"

"Why not? Some lucky guy might get a good night's sleep."

The sky was clear and dark when Paul met Jack on the ramparts that night. He walked along the wall from the center to the corner, overlooking the meadows on the north side of the fort, and Jack walked from the center to the opposite corner. Staring at the black meadows, faintly shadowed in the starlight, Paul thought he saw figures moving about.

"I think Indians are moving around out there," he reported when he met Jack at the center of the wall. Jack peered in the direction Paul was pointing. "I can't see nothing."

But with the first faint light of early dawn they could both see Indians running stealthily across the field to conceal themselves behind an entrenchment that had been raised in the night, from which they could fire upon the walls of the fort without exposing themselves.

"You must be able to see in the dark," Jack said, half amazed, half admiring. "Keep watching. I'm going to report this to the major right now."

"Ask him if I can go out with the patrol," Paul cried, as Jack climbed hastily down he ladder. "I saw them first!"

When Jack returned ten minutes later the sky was lightening slowly, and a gray light revealed the world outside.

"Major Gladwin sent for Lieutenant Hay and told him to take twenty men to wipe out that detachment out there. I told him the lookout who spotted it first wanted to go, and he said you'd earned the right. I've got a couple of men to take the rest of our watch. . . . Come on!"

He leaped to the ground and Paul followed. Two sleepy replacements were struggling up the ladder, and one of them grinned back at the two on the ground. "I'd rather be up here than out there," he said frankly. "Good luck!"

In high satisfaction, Paul marched out of the gate with Lieutenant Hay's patrol. This was the first time since the war had begun that he was joining the English in an attack upon the Indians. If they could capture some of the Indians, they could trade them for Captain Campbell. Paul felt the weight of his musket on his shoulder, and he felt very good indeed.

The entrenchment was a hundred yards from the fort, and the men advanced at the double-quick. Suddenly, when they were a dozen yards from the trench, a large number of Indians showed themselves upon the breastwork and fired a volley at the approaching patrol. Lieutenant Hay winced as if he'd been hit, and then, blood streaming down his arm, he raised his sword and ordered the charge, leading it at a headlong run.

Without warning, fear clutched Paul and stopped him cold. He wanted to turn and run, but even as his mind panicked, his feet chained him to one spot. The men ran past him, too intent on their goal to speak. He realized that he was going to be left behind, standing there alone, like a fool. This was even worse than being shot, so, gasping, he began to run after the soldiers. The fear subsided.

As the English charged up over the breastwork, Paul saw Jack leaping over the trench, following the fleeing Indians and firing as he ran. "I got one!" he yelled triumphantly. The rest of the English pursued the Indians, and there were too many of them between Paul and the Indians for him to fire.

He leaped up on the breastwork and began to tear at it with his bare hands, shamed and guilty because he

He leaped up on the breastwork and began to tear at it with his bare hands

had not been able to fire a single shot in his first battle. The other men began to return from the chase, and joined Paul in tearing down the breastwork.

In the field beyond, Jack was stooping over a dead Indian. His knife flashed in the dim light. He leaped to his feet and charged again toward the Indians, who had stopped a hundred yards away, waving a scalp with their own scalp yell. They watched him with ugly scowls. He waved the scalp again, jeeringly, and then turned and ran back to his own troops.

"That was a foolish thing to do," Lieutenant Hay told him sharply. "You've made them more angry than necessary, and they'll get their revenge."

Jack saluted with a wide smile. "I seen them do that to my friends, Lieutenant. I heerd them yell like that when they scalped the English. I just wanted to show them what it's like."

The lieutenant nodded, unsmiling, and told him to help fill in the trench. An hour later, they marched back to the fort. Jack showed Paul the scalp hung from his belt. "I'd ruther have this than a medal," he said proudly.

In mid-morning Major Gladwin called Lieutenant Hay's men to the parade ground to thank them for this successful action, and to reward them with leave for the rest of the day.

"I've been asked to announce at this time that the French within the fort want to form their own company," he went on. "All those who wish to belong to the French militia will meet here at once, to elect an officer to command the company."

Paul threw up his hat and cheered. Then he reddened as the English laughed at his enthusiasm. But the whole garrison cheered as Frenchmen moved onto the parade ground and lined up to count off. Paul stood beside his father. Henri was the third man in line, his chin thrust into the air, looking very sober. Paul looked down the line to see if Philippe might, perchance, have joined his family. But Philippe, with a group of French youths, was standing at the edge of the field, looking cynical.

The English garrison lined up facing the French company, and when the lines were formed Major Gladwin called for their attention again.

"This is an appropriate time to tell you of the final treaty of peace between France and England," he said. "Lieutenant Cuyler brought this news to me. The great war in Europe was officially ended on February 20, with the signing of this treaty in Paris."

He was interrupted with cheering, throwing of hats into the air, and cries of "Peace! Peace!" He smiled at the crowd, raised his hands for quiet, and went on. "It's a pity Pontiac could not have known that the great French Father will never return. But we, here in Fort Detroit, know now that Pontiac will gain no help from the forts in the Illinois country. France and England are now united in the new world."

The garrison saluted the new militia, and the militia

as cautiously as he himself would, he complained. Nonetheless, he responded to every requisition.

Philippe worked with his father, but his temper was becoming edgy, and Paul could see that he was irritable about staying in the fort. He wondered why Philippe stayed. Paul was more and more convinced that his brother had come home to aid Pontiac in some way from within the walls.

He could not mention this suspicion to his father, or to anyone: he had no proof. When he tried to think about the reason for his suspicion, he could tell himself only that Philippe had not joined the new company of militia, and that his brother was not the man he had admired for so long. Something was different between them, though Paul could not say why his feeling had changed, and he was saddened.

One day in late July, when Paul was working alone in the shop, Louis came in asking for Philippe.

"He went down to the arsenal to see the blacksmith . . . what do you want him for?"

"He's got the key to the gate; he borrowed it from me three days ago."

"Your key to the gate!" Paul's suspicions leaped up. "Why?"

Louis threw out his hands. "How would I know why? He said there was a girl on the south coast . . . it sounded reasonable enough. He said he'd return the key the next morning. My father was with the commandant at the time and Philippe couldn't wait. And I—well, anyway, I let him have the key." He buried his head in his hands, as if he felt guilty and stupid. "Now he hasn't returned it. My father goes to talk with the Ottawas this afternoon, and I can't tell him I let Philippe take his key! Would it be around here? Where did you say he has gone?"

"He's with the blacksmith . . . "

Blacksmith, Paul was thinking. Key to the fort. Philippe had spent most of the past three days with the blacksmith. He had wanted his parents to leave the fort because he thought the Indians were going to invade . . . Paul's heart pounded with his suspicions.

"You go to the blacksmith and see if he's still there," he said to his cousin. "I'll look around here."

He didn't want Louis to suspect what he himself was sure of.

Louis said hopelessly, "I hope I can find him, or that you can find that key somewhere. I'm in real trouble if I don't get it before this afternoon."

"We all are," Paul said to himself. But aloud he said, "It'll turn up. Give me an hour or so, and I'll find it."

Louis ran off, and Paul searched in the loft. There was nothing there, no place to hide anything. He ran back to the warehouse.

The key would be bulky and heavy. And it would be in some place where it would be unnoticed. His eyes roamed up the walls and across the raftered roof. It could be lying on one of those rafters, heavy and dark and high. He found a ladder and scrambled up to one of them, then crawled along the rafter from one end to the other. There was nothing.

He placed he ladder at the end of another rafter. Still, he found nothing. And then, as he turned and made his way back along the rafter to the end where he had left the ladder, he saw what he was looking for: lying out of sight on the beam that lay along the wall where it joined the roof, was the key Philippe had borrowed, and three copies.

The original key was easy to identify: it was made of bronze, while the copies were of iron. Paul brought them down, and laid the bronze key on the table to give to Louis as soon as his cousin returned. Steps sounded in the courtyard, and, frantic, he wheeled about, looking for a place to conceal the three copies. Quickly he thrust them in a dark corner behind six bags of flour, snatched up the bronze key, and ran back to the store.

Louis came in, winded, because he had run all the way up the hill.

"Monsieur Césire says Philippe hasn't been there to-day," he said sulkily. Then his eyes fell upon the bronze key on the counter. "Oh, you found it after all. Why didn't he just bring it back when he promised?"

Paul shrugged. "I don't know. He should have. Now he'll be angry when he finds it's gone . . ." He wished

Louis would leave. It made him nervous to have his cousin standing there looking cynical.

"Sometimes I wonder about Philippe," Louis remarked.

In angry defense, Paul became taut as a guy rope. "So?" he snapped. "What's wrong with Philippe?" He doubled his fists and scowled so ferociously that Louis backed away hastily.

"Oh, nothing—nothing at all!" he stammered. Then, clutching his key, he turned and ran.

Paul watched him moodily until he was out of sight. He saw Philippe and his father coming up the street, and he went back to the warehouse, where he picked up a broom and began sweeping. Three keys to the fort . . . the only purpose must be to unlock the gate. From the outside? The villainy of such a plan chilled him.

Philippe walked across the floor, looked at the ladder still standing at the end of the rafter where Paul had left it, and then stared thoughtfully at his brother. Paul ignored him, not raising his head, sweeping busily with the willow broom, as if that were the most important task of the day. Henri Girard looked in from the door of the store.

"Time for dinner," he said. He disappeared, and they could hear him shuttering and locking the window openings.

"Go ahead, Father," Paul called. "We'll be there as soon as we finish here."

Philippe leaned against the wall and watched Paul,

Paul ignored Philippe, continuing to sweep busily

his arms folded, his eyes wary. Paul, feeling his brother's eyes upon him, looked up and realized he had left the ladder where he had found the keys. He began to tremble. He thought about what he must say to his brother, and the strokes of the broom became slower and slower.

"Hurry up!" Philippe said impatiently. "You'll never get through in time for dinner."

Paul stopped, clutching the broom for support. He opened his mouth, but no sound came out. He felt strangled. Then he said, "Go ahead. Don't wait for me."

That wasn't what he had meant to say, and he felt stupid and young and helpless. Philippe was staring at him as if he were trying to hypnotize him.

Philippe's eyes shifted to the ladder. "You've got something on your mind," he said coldly.

Paul stopped again and pulled himself together. "I found the keys you had hidden," he said, tumbling his words out with a rush before his voice should fail him again. "You were going to betray this fort to Pontiac!"

"Where are they now?" Philippe demanded icily. He took a quick step toward Paul, and the younger boy dodged behind a barrel of powder.

"Listen to me, Philippe!"

"Pah! Why should I?"

"Because I can denounce you to Major Gladwin."

Philippe's eyes were burning with fury. "Why don't you, little rat?"

"Because . . ." Paul felt his voice shaking, and he

stopped a minute to steady it. "Because I hate to tell him my brother is a traitor. Perhaps—he doesn't have to know."

Philippe smiled, and in that smile he changed again into the warm, kindly brother Paul had always admired. "Of course he doesn't have to know," he said persuasively. "Give me the keys and forget it. Nothing will happen to my family."

Paul shook his head. "I won't have to tell the commandant if you leave the fort now. Today. And never come back. But if you don't leave today, Major Gladwin will know the whole story. And so will Father."

Philippe's eyes were black and icy and he stared at Paul murderously. Paul stared back, as angry as Philippe, and somehow no longer afraid of him. After a moment the older brother dropped his eyes and shrugged.

"Well enough," he said, as if the whole argument were of no importance, "we're late for dinner. Let us have no questions from our father."

"Of course," Paul agreed.

Philippe stalked into the dining room, sullen and silent. His mother said, "What is wrong, my son? Is something upsetting you?"

"He's angry because he had to take a barrel of powder down to the armory," his father said impatiently. "He behaves like a child."

Philippe reached for a chunk of bread. "I'm only angry with this stupid attitude of the French, that we must fight for the English at a time like this!" he cried explosively. "The Indians are our friends. So we must fight against them, beside the English who have always been our enemies. This is senseless. I will stay no longer, I tell you. I go to my friends, the Indians, tonight."

His father sprang to his feet and struck the table so the dishes clattered. "In this war we have no friends! I have told you before and I tell you again, it is madness to fight for the Indians."

"But you joined the militia under the Englishman Sterling," Philippe accused him. His face was contorted with anger. "This is our country, these lakes and woods. We were here a hundred years before the English. We've lived with the Indians like brothers, and now we should stand by, while the English drive out our friends and us, too? *This* is madness!"

"It is useless to resist," his father said coldly. "The French king has signed a treaty of peace with the English king, that they will fight no longer. This treaty binds us, too."

"No king speaks for me! I go back to my friends and the forest!"

He was gone, the door slamming behind him. Paul sprang to his feet. "I must speak to my brother before he goes!"

The streets were empty for these two hours while everyone—habitants and garrison alike—ate their midday dinner. Philippe strode through the narrow street, head up, chin thrust out. Paul, following a short distance behind, was sad.

He had always admired Philippe's courage, his gaiety, his wild, carefree life in the wilderness. He had envied the strength and skill Philippe had acquired from his Indian friends. And in the Indian camp Philippe was a different person. Paul felt like crying: he was losing an important part of himself, and already he felt an ache of emptiness.

As they passed the parade ground Philippe stopped to speak to someone. Paul drew closer and saw that it was Alexis. He dodged behind the corner of the nearest building and waited. Philippe clapped Alexis on the shoulder and went on to the gate, and Paul ran to catch up with him.

"Philippe!" he cried, and his voice broke, "let us part friends."

Philippe halted and looked back at the little brother who had always admired him. He smiled a little sadly, and waited while Paul came up to him.

"When the war is over, perhaps you can come home again," Paul said. He felt a hard knot closing his throat. It seemed, with Philippe gone, that no matter what happened, he himself would have lost the war.

"I don't know whether I'll ever come back," Philippe muttered.

He approached the sentry, spoke a few words, and the gate swung open. Paul watched, blinking to clear his eyes, until his brother had disappeared into the forest.

"He says he ain't coming back," the sentry observed, closing the gate and locking it securely. "Your brother, ain't he? Voyageur?"

Paul nodded. There was nothing to say.

"Well," said the sentry philosophically, "that's life for you. Come and go, come and go. Everything's bound to change. And then, on the other hand, he might come back with a load of goods, when the Injuns let the traders go through again."

Paul nodded, not caring to discuss it further, and turned toward his home. When he got back to the store his father was sleeping. Félice and the twins were squabbling about taking care of the cows. Suzette was cleaning up the lunch dishes. His mother was preparing to make bread.

Paul darted into the corner of the warehouse where he had hidden the three keys. They were still there, to his relief. He had been afraid that somehow or other they would have disappeared. It took him only a few minutes to dig a hole in a corner of the henyard, bury the keys twenty inches deep, and tramp down and cover the ground so no one could tell it had been disturbed.

Some day he might tell Major Gladwin. But not today. For now, he felt that not only had he saved the fort from disaster, but also his brother and his family from disgrace. For this he wanted no credit. All he really wanted was that his father should never know.

Chapter 15

WHEN Paul woke up the next morning, everything was quiet. It was already hot, and he lay sweating on his bed, thinking about the night before. What he had done gave him a deep sense of satisfaction. But mixed with the satisfaction was the memory of Philippe going away alone. Alone . . . Paul scowled as he realized that this meant Alexis was still in the fort. Alexis was like a rat, creeping out of corners when he was least expected, disappearing into some hole when you searched for him. . . . He smelled the eggs cooking for breakfast, he heard the hens cackling, and Suzette's light, quick voice talking to the cows as she milked them. It was time to be up and doing.

After breakfast he carried some laundry down to the waterfront for his mother. He stood at the water gate with the sentry for a few minutes, watching the women scrubbing their clothes on the rocks along the bank, with wooden paddles and soft, homemade soap. Marie Girard had found her favorite spot, where there was a big, rounded rock for scrubbing surface. She was talking to her neighbors while she worked.

The sentry winked at Paul. He liked to see the women

working on the waterfront. He said it made things seem kind of homey. Anchored in the river near the gate, the *Michigan* and the *Huron* stood with cannon trained upstream, downstream, and on the farther shore. Paul stared at the meadows across the river. The grass there was knee-high, feathery and undisturbed, and he thought wistfully of the lacrosse games that had trampled the grass a few weeks ago.

A canoe drew up at the landing place, and a Frenchman in a woodsman's cap and deerskin trousers climbed out. He was Monsieur Boileau, who lived in the forest near Parent's Creek, where he had cleared a little farm for himself. Sometimes he sent Henri Girard a few furs he had trapped during the winter. The women looked up with quick interest as he approached, and stopped talking. The Frenchman doffed his cap gallantly and called them flowers blooming on the waterfront. They giggled appreciatively, and he climbed on up the bank to the gate.

"Paul, my friend!"

The sentinel barred the gate with his musket.

"Monsieur Boileau is a friend of mine," Paul said.

The old woodsman pushed the musket aside as if it were the bar on a gate. "Show me to your friend, Monsieur Sterling."

The sentry scowled, and then shrugged and let him pass, as Paul nodded to him. Boileau took Paul by the arm. "I have a letter for Monsieur Sterling."

Paul walked up the sloping street toward Sterling's shop, glad to see an old friend and wondering cynically if this old friend was with the Indians now, like so many of the French outside the fort.

The Frenchman doffed his cap gallantly

"How are things with you?" he asked.

Boileau winked at him with great humor. "We're doing all right outside," he said, twisting his face into a comic expression. "The Indians, they want us to fight for them, they treat us like old friends. The English—Pah! They want food, they send to buy from us, we make money from them."

"Are you selling provisions to the fort?"

Boileau winked again. "But of course!" He gestured with both hands to show how generous he was. "Not all at once, you understand. You'll be glad one day that I held some back. When you need it more than you do now, you'll be glad there is still some flour with old Boileau, no?"

"I guess so. You said you had a letter for Monsieur Sterling?"

The jovial old habitant pulled out a scrap of paper from his greasy pocket and turned it over.

"See this?" He held it out, and Paul looked at it indifferently. It was crumpled and soiled, but folded together and properly sealed. "This is from an Englishman who is now a captive of the Ottawas."

Paul stopped. "What's his name? Is it Rutherfurd?"

Boileau nodded, laughing heartily. "These English names, who can pronounce them? Rutterfurd, that is right. Sterling is his friend, he says. Rutterfurd will give money to help himself escape, and Sterling will give more. So here is the letter to tell Sterling to pay me."

Paul stared at the letter as if he could read inside the folded, dirty scrap of paper. "Can you help him get away soon?"

"Oh, yes. Peewash is very fond of him; he treats him like a son. But lately the Indians have killed many English prisoners, and Rutterfurd thinks next time it might be him."

"You think you can help him escape?"

"But certainly! for money one can do almost anything."

The door of Sterling's shop stood open, and Paul could see him sitting at his desk looking at his accounts.

"No profit in this summer's trading!" he said, with a wry grimace, to his visitors. He pushed the account book to one side and came to the door. "What can I do for you?"

"Messenger with a letter for you, Captain Sterling. This is Monsieur Boileau from Parent's Creek."

Boileau handed over the letter, pulled off his greasy cap, and stood waiting while Sterling read the letter. Paul stepped outside the shop and lingered around until Boileau came out.

"I thought I'd better show you the way back to the river," he said. The Frenchman looked pleased.

"Good! In this fort I am not at home." He looked over his shoulder suspiciously at the Englishman, again seated at his desk. "Captain Sterling says he will pay me when Rutterfurd enters the fort. How can I tell he will give me the money?"

Paul was at once amused and irritated. "How can he tell you will deliver Rutherfurd, if you get the money first?"

Boileau's mobile face assumed a hurt expression. "But of course I will deliver the man! My faith, I know how unpleasant is captivity. My heart feels for him. I stand ready this instant..."

"So is Captain Sterling ready," Paul assured him. "The minute Rutherfurd is inside the gate of Fort Detroit you will have the money in your hands."

Boileau nodded sadly, as if it were painful to deal with such suspicion, but he was generous enough to overlook it.

"When can you bring him here?" Paul asked, as they approached the gate.

The Frenchman hunched his shoulders expressively. "Perhaps tonight. Perhaps tomorrow. Who knows how fate will manage these things?"

He climbed into his canoe and pushed off into the river without another word. The women watched him go and then began chattering about his errand. Paul walked slowly back to the garrison thinking of Rutherfurd's return. Possibly tonight...

He asked if he could stand the watch, hoping that if John should make his escape that night he might be the first to see him. The night was hot and sticky, and by midnight a heavy fog had settled over the terrain, as thick as milk, as white as snow. Nerves quickened. Paul thought, if the Indians chose to overrun the walls in this blanketing gloom, who would know until the hordes of savages were upon them? He gripped his gun more tightly and stared into the blank whiteness.

But through the long night nothing happened. As the night drew to an end, and the fog began to reflect the first faint glow of daylight, it thinned a little. And then in the eerie mist, barges began to show themselves, silent as ghosts.

"Look there," Tom Smith said to Paul, pointing downstream, "boats! But they couldn't be ours! Oh, no, that couldn't be for us! Must be Indians. Pass the word along to watch for an attack."

Paul started down the rampart walk to tell the next man the news, and before he reached him he heard a loud cheer from the river side of the wall. The whole garrison was collecting there, and Paul rushed to join them.

Half a dozen boats filled with red-coated English soldiers were approaching the water gate. As Paul watched, one after another followed the first six, slipping out of the fog into the line.

It was the reinforcement from Niagara, twenty-two boats with two hundred and sixty men, food and ammunition. Paul counted them incredulously. Why, the war must be over!

The habitants, wakened by the cheering and the firing, filled the streets. Paul's father carried a flaring torch, and the firelight fell on the white hair of an aged grand-mother and the laughing faces of Félice and the twins, as they capered and danced with excitement.

The captain of the new contingent met Major Glad-win, and Paul could hear them clearly.

"You are to be congratulated, Captain Dalyell," Major Gladwin told him. "These waterways are infested with hostile Indians now. It's a miracle you weren't attacked and overwhelmed."

Captain James Dalyell lifted his handsome blond head as if he felt invincible. "Luck sailed with us all the way, Major Gladwin. This fog hung over the river all the way from Lake Erie. We did have fourteen men wounded as we passed the Huron camp back there. But otherwise no interference at all. I'm anxious to have at the scoundrels."

He sounded like John Rutherfurd, Paul thought: the same confidence, the same excitement about hunting out danger and facing it down, the same assurance that life would treat him well. He wondered when John was going to make his escape, and then put the thought aside, as the new captain and the commandant began to walk toward the commandant's house.

"I suggest a surprise attack, as soon as the men have rested," Captain Dalyell was saying. "All the way up the river I was afraid the Indians might be scared off when they saw these reinforcements for the fort . . ." He laughed. "I'm still afraid Pontiac will give up the siege and slink off into the forest before I can meet him in battle and beat him properly. The thing is to surprise him."

The major said drily, "It would be impossible to surprise these Indians, my dear captain. They're not fools, you know."

Captain Dalyell looked skeptical. "But we must seize the offensive with these savages before they expect us to strike."

They moved out of earshot, and Paul went back to the ramparts thinking soberly about the young captain.

Chapter 16

O N the evening of July 30 all the troops assembled on the parade ground for instruction. The entire population of the fort came out to watch them, crowding the streets and bickering with the sergeants at arms, who kept pushing the civilians off the parade ground to get them out of the way of the troops.

The sun glared low and hot over the west stockade. Heat rose from the dusty ground, but in the excitement no one noticed the discomfort. Dalyell's troops were going to make a surprise attack on Pontiac's Indian forces the next night, and everyone knew about it.

On the parade ground the new redcoats were forming their companies. Spruce and energetic, they stepped smartly around, pleased to show these tired and dowdy garrison men how soldiers should perform. Weapons were distributed. Sabers and ammunition were passed out to the new troops. And one of their officers called out orders for the coming attack.

Paul stood stiffly in line with the French militia, turning his eyes sideways from time to time to watch the new officers and men. Somewhere in the crowd he saw a Frenchman laughing. He focused his attention more closely. The man turned a little, and Paul saw him clearly: it was Alexis Cuillerier.

Impulsively he took a step, prepared to break and run, to hold his cousin. He caught Captain Sterling's eye, forbidding any motion. Red with embarrassment, he pulled back into line and stood straighter than usual, while the British officer announced, "We shall make a sortie tomorrow, probably around two in the morning. Check weapons, powder, and ammunition. Be ready to assemble at the first call, in complete quiet, or the surprise will be lost."

Paul's eyes went back to the spot where he had seen Alexis. There was no sign of him. The order came to break ranks. He darted from the line, ran squarely into James Sterling and knocked him to the ground.

Embarrassed beyond speech, Paul slid to a stop and turned to help his captain to his feet again. Captain Sterling looked angry, which he seldom did.

"Why do you dash around like a chicken with your head off?" he snapped.

"My deepest apologies," Paul said, standing very formally before him. "I saw a spy . . ." He looked about, not wanting anyone to overhear him.

"Ah!" Captain Sterling turned and looked across the parade ground. "Where is he now? Did he hear the directions for the attack?"

"He must have. But he has disappeared . . . " Paul was dancing with impatience to run after Alexis.

"I'll send directions to stop him at the gates," said Captain Sterling.

"Let me tell the sentries at the water gate," Paul begged.

The captain nodded. "Tell them to let no Frenchman go through."

Paul turned and ran. "Captain Sterling's orders!" he shouted, as he came within range of the sentry at the water gate. "Let no Frenchman go through the gates till further notice."

The sentries saluted. Paul came up to the closing gates, and asked, breathless, "Has any Frenchman left the fort by this gate tonight?"

"None here," the sentry said.

He returned to the parade ground, walking around the wall from gate to gate. The order had reached all sentries, but they were uncertain as to whether any Frenchman had left the fort before the order came. Slowly Paul went back to report to Captain Sterling. If Alexis had left the fort with his information about Captain Dalyell's plans, it would be disastrous.

Paul stood his watch that night. The warm wind was blowing from the west; the pale moon was bright and full in the sky, as he watched Captain Dalyell lead his troops to battle at two-thirty in the morning.

Captain Sterling had sent Paul's message to Major Gladwin and told Paul what the mayor had replied. "Captain Dalyell thinks there is no problem," he said, looking sardonic. "Major Gladwin has been advising him since his arrival not to be over-confident and hasty. But the captain is convinced he knows more about Indian fighting than we do."

The soldiers moved in double file through the west gate, sabers gleaming in the moonlight, and bayonets shining jauntily. They turned right as they left the gate, and marched up the river road, two abreast. While Paul watched, the line stretched out and out, a long snake of glinting steel and tramping feet, until the leaders disappeared into the shadows of the forest. No man spoke, but the muffled tramp of feet and the rattle of arms could not be stilled.

Two miles from the fort a narrow wooden bridge crossed Parent's Creek, in front of Baptiste Meloche's house. Beyond the bridge, Dalyell expected to find Pontiac and all his braves sleeping, and planned to surprise and slaughter all of them.

Two gunboats accompanied the line of fighting men, each boat mounting a swivel gun to cover the attack from the water. As the last of the line went through the gate of the fort, Paul began to tighten up with apprehension. He wanted to talk to the man next to him, and found that he couldn't. All he could do was listen. And the longer he waited, the more fearful he became.

The last man had disappeared and the night was quiet and empty, clearly lighted by the full moon. Paul leaned against the stockade, his eyes fixed on the blackness of the forest. A crash of musket fire sounded. He jumped and stood rigid. The sound was repeated and became continuous. Above the gunfire he heard screams. Then he heard the Indian war whoops and scalp yells.

The men beside Paul shook their heads somberly. "Those blasted Injuns knew they was coming," one of them muttered. "They got Captain Dalyell trapped."

The sentry in charge said, "To your posts, men. No telling when they might try an assault on the fort from the other side."

The men went back to the other walls, and Paul stood alone, staring at the moonlit field below and thinking—about Philippe, about Alexis, about John Rutherfurd. He dropped his head on his arms and shuddered. The firing went on and on, and so did the scalp yells. The worst of all was the Indian victory yell that sounded every once in awhile.

Amid the noise and the cries and the yelling, the night dragged endlessly. In the moonlight, Paul saw one of the gunboats moving downriver toward the fort. It approached the gate and the sentry gave the customary challenge.

"Lieutenant Abbot with wounded from the battle."

A dozen soldiers ran down to the water line to carry the wounded ashore. The lieutenant walked as if exhausted. To one of the garrison he said, "They need ammunition out there. Can you load the boat as soon as the men are taken off?"

"What happened, sir?"

"The Indians ambushed us. There must be four hundred out there. I don't know how we'll come out of this . . . someone told them we were coming!" His voice jangled with outrage. "Captain Dalyell was killed . . ."

"Captain Dalyell!" The men looked at each other.

The young lieutenant left his wounded men groaning and cursing on pallets on the floor of the church and started back up the river with a boat loaded with barrels of powder and shot. And at eight that morning the men who had marched out so gallantly less than six hours before came back to the fort limping, angry, and heartsick. Besides Captain Dalyell, one sergeant and eighteen of their comrades had been killed, three officers and thirty-nine men wounded.

"How many Indians were lost?" Paul asked Louis, when he found him on the parade ground as the men came through the gate. Louis shook his head.

"Nobody knows for sure. Some of the men thought maybe seven were killed and a dozen wounded, but nobody knows." He shook his head again. "Indians always manage not to lose many of their men," he said, admiring the Indian strategy objectively. "My father says everyone warned Captain Dalyell a surprise wouldn't work, but he wouldn't listen. . . Do you know what Lieutenant Abbot calls Parent's Creek now?"

"What did he say about it?"

"He calls it Bloody Run. The water was running red

during the battle, from the blood of men that fell in—"

Paul sighed. "I'm going home for awhile," he muttered. He felt as tired as if he had fought in that battle himself, as guilty as if he himself had betrayed the foolhardy young captain.

Stoically the garrison settled down after Dalyell's defeat to continue holding on. The French militia under Captain Sterling drilled on the parade ground daily, and shared the night watch with the garrison. Everyone knew a French spy had been responsible for the defeat at Bloody Run, and the French were more loyal now than at any time since the beginning of the war, trying to make up for that disaster.

A week had gone by since old Boileau had brought his letter to James Sterling, and Paul wondered if John had tried to escape and been caught. And then he tried not to think about him at all. But he found himself waking up from sleep in a cold sweat, dreaming of seeing Rutherfurd lying on the floor of an Indian tepee, his skull crushed with a tomahawk, his scalp dangling in the hand of a grinning savage.

On Friday after the defeat at Bloody Run, Paul dreamed again of John slaughtered, and he woke with a sense of deep melancholy. He got out of bed slowly and wearily and ate his breakfast without appetite, which distressed his mother.

"My boy, you must not be well," she said, filling his plate with corn cakes for the third time.

He pushed the plate back, irritated with her worry. But he said nothing. This was a free day for him, and he should be gay. What was there to be gay about? he demanded angrily of himself. He went into the street and looked out over the stockade at the world outside. It looked so green and spacious, so free, after these weeks of being cooped up. The schooner *Huron* lay at anchor across from the gate and, as Paul watched, he saw they were preparing to bring a man from the ship to the fort. He ran down to the gate to see who this might be.

He was a dirty, greasy, painted old Indian, with swollen legs. A prisoner, possibly, who could be exchanged? The canoe crossed the stretch of water, and the Indian climbed painfully out upon the sandy beach. Paul stiffened in wild excitement. It was John Rutherfurd!

John walked slowly across the sandy strip to the gate. His legs were twice as big as normal, and had been torn and scratched by thorns and briars. His face was covered with red, black, and green paint. When Paul looked again, he wondered how he knew it was Rutherfurd. But the youth grinned at him and cried, "Paul! Am I glad to see you!"

"So you did get away!" Paul's throat choked up and he had to swallow and cough before he could talk again. The streets were filling with people who had

John walked slowly across the sandy strip to the gate

heard that an escaped captive had returned, and as John walked up the narrow street toward James Sterling's house, the crowd cheered and waved. He walked slowly and painfully, but his eyes were glistening with happiness.

"Why didn't old Boileau come in with you?" Paul asked. "I saw him when he brought your note to Mr. Sterling a week ago."

"He brought me to the *Huron* at night, and then he was afraid the Indians would know he'd helped me escape, if he didn't get back. He said they'd scalp him for sure if they found out."

So old Boileau had trusted Rutherfurd and his English friends, after all. Paul felt better about the habitants when he thought about that. He learned later that Mr. Sterling sent the promised money to old Boileau the very day John returned.

"It was your brother who helped me get away to Boileau, in the end," John said, smiling at Paul. "He looked me up after the battle of Bloody Run."

Paul nodded, deeply pleased with Philippe, but unable to say anything about it. John looked harder and more sober than when he had left, Paul thought. But the old spirit of adventure was as lively as ever.

"They treated me well," he reported of his captivity, some days later. "When Peewash knew the braves were sacrificing prisoners, he hid me or I should never have lived so long. But they were cruel to some of the others."

He looked sad. "I'll never forget poor Davers. So happy with his chance to explore the lakes, so sure he was a friend of the Indians, because he spoke some of their languages. They didn't even give him a chance to speak . . ."

He turned to Paul, and his eyes blazed with the same excitement that had burned there before the ill-fated trip.

"When I came out here I wanted to see the wilderness, you know. These forests are so exciting, so untouched, so primitive, so new and so endless! There's a job to be done here, and I want to stay. I'd like to fight for Fort Detroit, or at any other spot where I'm needed."

A week later he signed on with the crew of the *Michigan* to get supplies from Niagara for the garrison.

"But others can do that," Paul protested. "Why go into Indian country again? There's not a fort between here and Niagara that hasn't fallen to the Indians! You don't want to fight them again?"

Rutherfurd laughed, a wide, joyous laugh that showed all his white teeth. "One fort still stands." He held up one finger. "Fort Pitt is still there. And Sterling needs someone to oversee his cargo on this trip. I told him I'd be glad to do it. After all—" he spoke as easily as if he anticipated a pleasure cruise—"I'm used to Indians now."

Chapter 17

THE month of August went by with tedious minor assaults and no results. The fort was stronger, since Dalyell's party had arrived, in spite of the disastrous attack at Parent's Creek. For both sides, the siege had settled into a matter of holding on.

The September days wore on, slow and warm and beautiful. The leaves turned crimson on the oak trees, the birches stood white and gold among the black-green spruces, the maples glowed scarlet. And the beautiful days passed into October.

"This can't go on forever," Paul said to Jack Bradshaw, as they stood on the ramparts and looked at the brilliant forest. He was beginning to feel as if he'd lived under siege all his life, as if the war would never end.

"I'll be glad when my army time is up," the Englishman said. "I'm ready to settle down and start building."

"Here?" Paul was astonished. Only six weeks ago Jack had been impatient to return to England.

"Sure. This is going to be a great country. There's always going to be something to fight for here."

"You like fighting?" Paul raised his eyebrows.

"Why not? You don't ever stop fighting." Jack stood

his musket on end and looked at Paul. "Mebbe the army stops, but a man doesn't. If it isn't the Injuns, it'll be something else . . ." He laughed. "This wild country here, it'll take more trouble, but we'll have more freedom. This will be a good life, once we get rid of the Injuns." He looked far away, across the river and the meadows. "A good life," he repeated.

His comrade on the other side of Paul looked at him as if Jack were out of his mind. "I wouldn't miss this country one minute," he declared, scowling at the forest. "Just let me out of here, once!"

Paul left them arguing and went down to the river bank. Sometimes the men talked hopefully of Pontiac's giving up and leaving them alone any day now. But a soldier had ventured out just the day before, and had been killed before the eyes of the garrison by a shot from an unseen gun in the forest. After that, no one was reckless enough to believe the siege was ended.

A canoe full of voyageurs passed up the river toward Lake St. Clair, whence it would go north through Lake Huron into the north woods waters. The men sang as they drove their paddles into the water, and suddenly the hunger to run free and wild in that outside world struck Paul's heart like an arrow, and he winced with longing.

He thought of Philippe, for the first time in weeks, and a sense of melancholy enwrapped him. He stared up the river, whence the canoe had disappeared, and remembered the good days when the French, the English, and the Indians had lived together in peace. He longed to see his brother again. He remembered the day Philippe had left the fort, never to return. But more clearly he recalled the warmth and laughter and heroic tales of the days when Philippe was at home.

He looked around the ramparts. For months now he had been shut up in this little fort, and the walls seemed to press upon him. If he found Philippe, if he went off with him this winter into the wilderness, what difference would it make to anyone? Except that he, Paul, would again be living that wild, free life that he loved so much. He sprang to his feet and ran to Captain Sterling's shop.

The boy saluted. "Captain Sterling, I'd like your permission to leave the fort, sir."

The captain of the militia glanced at him as if his mind were on other problems. "Why?"

"I'd like to see my brother again. And perhaps I could find out how much longer the Indians will stay with the siege."

"That might be a good thing. Talk to Major Gladwin."

The major was working on a report for his superiors at Niagara, when Paul was admitted. He looked tired, but patient and durable, as if he could spend the rest of his life in this fort holding Pontiac at bay. Paul explained his request.

"Possibly you could find out something useful," the major agreed. He got up and strode back and forth, thinking aloud. "The Potawatomies from Fort St. Joseph came to me last week to make peace. They said some of the other tribes were tired of the long war. I'd like to know more about this. See what you can do, Paul. Any information you can bring back will be helpful."

He sat down and picked up his quill again, to scribble a pass for the boy. "Take care," he said, handing Paul the pass.

Paul approached the Ottawa village in darkness. He

The chief was in council with his braves. In the open

heard Pontiac speaking, and he crept behind the tepees where he could listen. The chief was in council with his braves. In the open circle in the midst of the encampment, the council fire threw a flickering light on the dark faces turned toward Pontiac.

"Manitou, the Ottawa chief, has left you," a brave cried angrily. "He is tired of this war, he wants to hunt now."

Pontiac turned his hawk-like face toward the speaker. "Let Manitou go! Pontiac can fight without him."

"Wasson has gone to the fort to make peace," cried

circle, the fire threw a flickering light on the dark faces

another. "Our women and children are hungry, we have no food. Let us forget the fort for the winter. The English will not run away! In the spring we can fight again."

The braves stirred restlessly. "Who will feed our families all winter?"

Pontiac raised a hand. "We can cut off the supplies from the fort, we can starve them and feed ourselves at the same time."

"But we have not cut off the supplies before this!"

Paul crawled away from the wrangling council and made his way toward his brother's tepee. As he raised the deerskin flap and appeared in the narrow opening, Philippe's head jerked up. He was sitting alone beside a tiny fire in the center of the tepee. Paul stepped inside and crouched over the fire opposite him.

"What are you here for?" Philippe demanded.

"You'll be going to hunt soon, and I wanted to see you before you left."

"I thought you never wanted to see me again," Philippe said coldly.

Paul felt as if a wall stood between him and Philippe. "I saw some voyageurs going up the river this afternoon," he said in a low voice. It was not easy to talk to Philippe in this mood. "I got thinking about the wilderness. I'm tired of the fort, and I thought about your going and . . . I guess I just wanted to see you again."

The older brother glanced at the younger, and some of

the old warmth came into his eyes. "My friends are the Indians, now and always," he reminded him.

"Sometimes I wonder if anyone cares, or if it matters," Paul said, looking into the coals. "The English still hold the fort. Pontiac will never drive them out. But maybe it doesn't matter any more whether I stay there or not."

Philippe looked at him sharply, and a smile began to show in his eyes. "Would you like to go with me this winter?"

Paul looked at him, astounded. "You mean you'd take me with the voyageurs—this year?"

"I think you could be one, yes."

"The kings have signed the treaty of peace," Paul said, as if he were thinking out loud. "We're all bound to obey the English rulers now." But if he went with the voyageurs, he would be free, as the wilderness men were free.

"I will not be bound by some far-off king," Philippe said violently. "But I'm through with the war, anyway. I'm tired of it, and when I see a thing is impossible I prefer to forget it. I'm ready now to fight with bears, winds, snow, rushing water . . ." He stood and stretched his mighty shoulders. "This fighting the English, pah! For what? For a little fort too small to hold me . . ."

"Where is Alexis now? Has he joined the Indians?"

Philippe shook his head indifferently. "After the battle of Parent's Creek he stayed with me a night. He knew he could never return to the fort, and he was going toward the Illinois country. He said he had friends there."

"Is he plotting any more trouble?"

Philippe raised an eyebrow. "Who knows? But it's too late for this year. The Indians are going to hunt any day now. Alexis hates the English too much to stay here. He'd rather be in the Illinois country where the French still command their own forts."

"Will Pontiac fight on, do you think?"

Philippe crouched again by the fire. "He can't fight after the snow flies. Even now his braves talk of hunting . . . . Well, what say you? Will you leave your English friends and be a wilderness man with me?"

Would he? Now Paul wasn't sure, though for years this had been his dream. He said slowly, "I'll sleep in your tepee tonight and tell you tomorrow." Philippe nodded, as if it meant little to him.

When he woke in the morning, Paul looked at his brother cooking the cornmeal over the breakfast fire. With Philippe he would fight the bears and winds and weather in the wilderness. His English friends would not criticize him if he went voyaging with his brother. He thought of Jack Bradshaw building his log cabin, plowing his farm, watching his apple trees bloom in the spring. He thought of his father's store and of the place his father wished him to take, of the studies in Montreal Father Bocquet urged upon him. He thought of the Indians, free and wild, the life he had always believed he loved. And he thought of the courage that took Englishmen through hostile territory to Niagara, back and forth, again and again. He thought of Captain Campbell: "A Campbell gave his word and a Campbell keeps it." He thought of John Rutherfurd going into Indian territory ten days after he had escaped from captivity. He thought of Major Gladwin. Some time, he hardly knew when, he had realized that the courage of these brave men was more admirable than anything Philippe had ever done. The challenge of the New World was more exciting now than the challenge of the wilderness.

To live peacefully in that New World, he must work with the Indians and the English, not fight them. He would go to Montreal and get the schooling Father Bocquet wanted him to have. And he began to wonder how soon he could set out. Suddenly the big city of Montreal looked more exciting, even, than the wilderness.

He faced his brother and he felt, for the first time, that he was a man. "The forest is your destiny and the fort is mine," he said, trying to speak as lightly as the English spoke of their decisions. "I'll go back."

Philippe's eyes narrowed. Something in Paul's manner surprised him and aroused his respect. "As you will."

"But when you return in the spring, will you bring furs to the Girard trading post?" Paul was wistful in spite of himself.

Philippe looked at him with the old, flashing smile Paul loved. "But of course!"

The leaves fell from the trees, the color faded from the forests, and the days grew shorter, darker, and colder. On October 29 the ground froze hard, and snow fell all day, four inches deep. The garrison lighted fires on the parade ground, to warm hands and feet during sentry duty, and talked about spending the rest of the winter under arms. Paul's mother was getting his clothes in order for the trip to Montreal. The *Huron* would sail as soon as the Indians left for their winter's hunting. Some day they *must* leave, the men told each other. But they were beginning to think Pontiac could withstand even a winter without food.

The next day word swept around the fort that a letter had arrived from Pontiac for the major. The habitants dashed to his house, huddled in blankets and blowing on their fingers, to hear the news.

When he saw the waiting, hopeful people, Major Gladwin's stony face broke into a wide smile. He waved to them, and stepped upon a high rock, to tell them the good news. "Pontiac has given up the siege. Now hear this letter.

My Brother,

The word which my father has sent me to make peace I have accepted; all my young men have buried their hatchets. I think you will forget the bad things which have taken place for some time past. Likewise I shall forget what you may have done to me, in order to think of nothing but good. I, the Chippewas, the Hurons, we are ready to go speak with you when you ask us. Give us an answer. I am sending this resolution to you in order that you may see it. If you are as kind as I, you will make me a reply. I wish you a good day.

PONTIAC.

The French looked at each other, laughed and cried, and then, catching hands, they danced in the streets. As Paul watched them, gay with their gaiety, the song of the voyageurs fell upon his ears. He turned and ran to the water gate.

A great canoe was moving downstream at full speed, and the song of thirty voyageurs sounded across the water, as the paddles rose and fell in unison. As the canoe passed the fort, one man held his paddle aloft, as if he signaled.

Philippe! Paul thought. He tore off his fur cap and waved. The voyageur raised and lowered his paddle, and then fell into stroke with the others. Paul scrambled up to the top of the bastion, to watch them out of sight.

As the canoe dwindled in the distance, he felt as if some spell had been lifted from him. No longer did he crave the wilderness struggle of the voyageurs, and instead he felt as if he had caught up with his brother, but in his own way. He sent a ringing shout down the river following the canoe, and in the distance a single paddle stood aloft again, and the craft disappeared behind a forest darkness along the faraway bank.

He turned from the river and saw the Indians crossing the meadow. Pontiac was leading his village out to the winter hunt. Paul watched them go as they had gone for centuries, the squaws carrying the tepees, the braves carrying the guns. All winter they would range the forests, cold, hungry, surviving, returning. But some day when the white men had built their towns, the forests would no longer yield game. Paul knew this was what the Indians fought, in vain.

Otussa looked up as the straggling band moved past, and waved to his friend. Paul waved back, wondering as he did so when he would see Otussa again, when they could be friends again. And slowly the Indians filed into the trees to the north and out of sight.

Author's Note

THE HISTORY in this story is true. It all happened two hundred years ago, and most of the characters in my story are true, also. The Girards and Louis La Butte are people of my imagination. But the Navarres, who had a wedding for their daughter, Marie-Francoise, were living on the south coast, outside the fort, in 1763, and the man she married was the English officer, George McDougall. Her father, Robert Navarre, kept a diary of the siege. Angélique Cuillerier, the daughter of old Antoine, heard about Pontiac's plot in her father's house and warned the English, because she feared for the life of her sweetheart, James Sterling, the English trader. Two years after the siege she married him. All the French in this story are historical figures except the Girards, and most of them have descendants still living in Detroit today.

Because these people were born in the New World, they considered themselves "French-Canadian." Some had come to Detroit from Montreal and Quebec, some had been born in the little settlement on the Detroit River. I have called them French, because that was their language. They also called themselves "habitants" which, in their own tongue, meant "settlers."

The English officers and traders were historical people, too, except for Jack Bradshaw and Tom Smith, soldiers in the garrison. Sir Robert Davers was a middle-aged British tourist, who has become historical because of his part in the Rutherfurd expedition. John Rutherfurd, who was in Detroit in 1763 at the age of seventeen, has left his own story of his captivity, which happened as I have told it in this story.

The habitants believed that disaster was forecast by the strange "black rain" that actually fell in October, before the Indian uprising in May of 1763.

Most of the French spoke English as well as some of the Indian tongues; hence they could converse in French with each other or in English with Englishmen. I have not tried to indicate the use of any special language at any time, since all were used so generally. Where possible I have used Pontiac's own words, which have been recorded as part of history. His speech in Chapter 5, where he is in council with Major Gladwin and Captain Campbell, and his letter in Chapter 17 are historical statements.

There was more action and excitement than has been possible to include in the story of Paul Girard's summer under siege. Pontiac did return to try again the following year. If you want to read the real history of this event, Francis Parkman has told it completely and stirringly in his *History of the Conspiracy of Pontiac*.

PRINTED IN U.S.A.

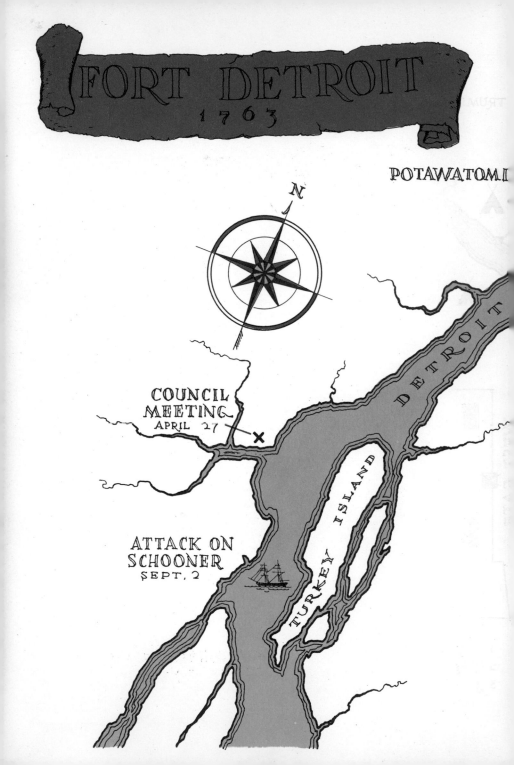